ALMOST PERFECT

DELANEY DIAMOND

GARDEN AVENUE PRESS

1

S able Devereaux slipped quietly through the shadows and approached the house with a backpack strapped to her back, almost invisible in an all-black cat suit and black shoes on her feet.

The grand estate with a gated entrance was enclosed behind a ten-foot-high wall in the French countryside. Sable glanced around to ensure she wasn't being watched, though she didn't expect to be, due to the few houses in the area.

She ran toward the wall and pressed her foot a couple of feet up, propelling her body higher. Hands covered in black gloves gripped the rough edge at the top and protected her fingers.

She pulled herself up and rested flat on her stomach to survey the darkness. Trees and shrubs cast shadows on the property, but all around was mostly quiet except for the typical night sounds. The guests were already inside, enjoying the dinner party thrown by wealthy businessman Jean-Jacques Moreau.

An antique dealer with multiple stores, in recent years rumors emerged that he engaged in more questionable lines of work, though he'd never been convicted of a crime. Perhaps he hired the best lawyers in the land, but Sable suspected he simply knew the right people to bribe. Exactly the kind of person she had no qualms about stealing from.

There were no dogs on the property except a terrier belonging to Moreau's wife, a pampered pooch that stayed inside and which a magazine did an entire spread on. Ridiculous. Security kept an eye on the outside cameras directed at the front and back of the mansion. She would enter from the blind spot on the side.

Sable dropped to the grass below.

The Moreaus liked to entertain, and tonight's lavish dinner party meant they'd be preoccupied with their guests, and there'd be no alarms to set off. Entering the house would be easy. She ran over to the wall and took one more look around before slipping a mask over her head. Then she began her ascent.

Years of practice meant effortlessly finding footholds and handholds in the stone exterior, which allowed her to scale the side as easily as going up an indoor rock-climbing wall.

She moved silently and slowly, holding on with fingers strengthened over the years. She gripped a window ledge and boosted higher. Braced her foot against a downspout and lifted higher still. By the time she reached the third-floor balcony, her heart rate had not increased much, but excitement flushed her skin at having reached the top and closer to the prize within.

Testing the door, she found it locked, but thanks to the tools in her backpack, within seconds she unlocked the door. She entered the dark office where Moreau conducted his business when he didn't go in to his office at his company headquarters. She waited until her eyes adjusted to the low light and then crept across the carpet, careful not to make any noise.

She'd known about the man's obsession with George Washington but was still unprepared for all the memorabilia. Images of Washington and letters he'd written covered one wall. As a history buff, she understood the importance of these objects and their value. Hundreds of thousands of dollars' worth of history hung on the walls and was displayed in cases.

But that's not why she'd come. There was a bigger prize available.

Sable went over to the portrait of Moreau hanging on the wall. He stood erect, large nose tilted toward the ceiling, dark eyes looking down at her as if in judgment. She involuntarily shivered. The man gave her the creeps.

She set the painting on the floor, and excitement flooded her veins when she saw the small safe behind it. This one would be a piece of cake, employing simple lock manipulation —the purest form of safe-cracking.

Sable wiggled her fingers and went to work. Ear pressed to the safe, she used her senses—touch, sight, sound—turning the dial and lining up the numbers into the grooves. Less than five minutes later, she pulled down on the lever, and the door popped open to reveal her ticket to freedom—the complete first volume of a Gutenberg Bible resting on a white pillow. Her knees went weak, and she grinned like someone who'd been handed a blank check. Years of successfully slipping in and out of homes under the cover of darkness led her to this moment.

She ignored an external drive and eyed the stack of euros beside it. She hadn't come for the money, but she'd take the cash. The Bible, however, was worth millions.

She stuffed the bills into the front pocket of the backpack and then carefully lifted out the Bible. "Come to Mama."

Raised voices on the opposite side of the door gave her pause and made her blood pressure spike. At least two people —both male—were coming closer, which meant she had to get out of there.

Darn it. Who were they, and why weren't they downstairs with the guests?

Moving fast, she closed the safe and lifted the portrait back on the wall. Running on her toes, she hurried toward the balcony, but the door behind her pushed open. With no time to slip out, Sable dashed behind the heavy curtains near a window. She pressed her back to the wall, but the backpack with the Bible and tools made it impossible to get completely flat. She sucked in her stomach as the light came on.

The people continued to argue.

"You've gotten greedy," a gravelly voice said in French.

Sable placed her eye to the slit between the two drapes and saw a large bearded man dressed in a suit. From previous surveillance, she recognized him as one of Moreau's security.

A man with graying black hair glared up at him, his face vaguely familiar.

"What are you going to do, Bertrand? Your job is to follow orders. You're nothing but a big dumb animal."

Oh boy.

Bertrand became red-faced and looked angry enough to crush rocks with his teeth. He sized up the smaller man with insolent appraisal. "And you're nothing but a whore willing to sell his soul for a few euros."

The smaller man sputtered in anger, and Bertrand back-handed him.

The slap landed hard, and the smaller man stumbled out of her line of sight. The blow was so sudden Sable emitted a soft gasp and clamped a hand over her mouth, freezing and trying to press farther into the wall. Fortunately, they didn't hear her.

"You always have your hand out, begging for more," Bertrand said with disgust.

He walked out of view, and the door clicked closed.

"Wh-what are you doing?"

She held her breath, the same fear in the smaller man's voice causing a swirl of unease in her lower belly.

"There's been a change of plans. Mr. Moreau no longer

wishes to do business with you, and there are plenty of others who can take your place."

Sable rubbed her suddenly itchy nose. Surely she wasn't about to sneeze at this moment.

"I wanted to speak to him privately—"

"We know why you wanted to speak with him privately. To beg for more money, but your services are no longer needed."

"If that's so, then let me go."

"I'm afraid I can't." Bertrand prowled into view.

"Please." The smaller man's voice shook, his terror evident. Sable swallowed hard.

"I'm sorry. It's just business," Bertrand said.

He lunged, and then Sable heard muted gasping. Using one finger, she eased aside the drapes and stared wide-eyed at the big man choking the much smaller one. She scanned the room for a weapon and settled on one of the framed George Washington letters hanging on the wall. If she could sneak from behind the drapes, get the framed document, and hit the big guy on the back of the head, she could save this poor man.

She was about to try when the door cracked open, and Mr. Moreau stepped into the room. Sable didn't move another inch.

Moreau wore a black tux and a bored expression. He closed the door and watched dispassionately as his security guard choked the life out of another man. The victim clawed frantically at Bertrand's beefy arms, to no avail. His lips and face turned blue. He wheezed as he struggled for air.

Sable bit her lip. She should do something, but if they discovered her, she was as good as dead. Her nose itched again, and she rubbed it with the back of her thumb.

Finally, the victim's arms fell to his sides, and the room went quiet.

Bertrand let him drop to the floor.

Moreau shook his head. "Greed is one of the seven deadly sins for a reason. Clean this mess up."

"Yes, sir."

Moreau exited the room.

Bertrand moved out of sight, whistling a tune, as if he hadn't just murdered someone. Sable couldn't believe what she'd seen.

Then a black cat sauntered into view and stared right at her. "Meow."

She stiffened. *Oh no.*

That's why her nose itched. She knew about the dog but didn't know the Moreaus owned a cat. He must be a new pet. The darn animal must have slipped into the office with Bertrand.

The cat meowed again and strolled toward her, tail pointing at the ceiling. *No, no, no, no.* Her breathing became jagged as alarm blazed through her.

He came right over and rubbed up against her ankle.

No! Sable screamed inside her head.

Despite the drapes providing a barrier, their close proximity proved too much. Water sprang to her eyes, and then... she sneezed.

She froze, hoping Bertrand hadn't heard. No such luck. Seconds later, he yanked aside the drapes.

His eyes widened in disbelief. "Who are you?" he demanded in French.

Sable kneed him in the groin, and he howled, grabbing his crotch. She sidestepped him, but not fast enough. He stretched one long arm, grabbed her backpack, and yanked her backward. She tumbled to the ground, and the cat scampered away.

Sable sneezed twice, then rolled onto all fours.

Breathing heavy and stooped over in pain, the big man demanded, "Who the hell are you?"

Sable sneezed again and did the only thing she could think of. She shot to her feet and charged him, throwing all her weight into his body. They crashed against the wall, but he cuffed her neck with brutally strong fingers. He was bigger and stronger, but she had agility on her side. She twisted and slipped from his grasp, but his fingers gripped the mask to hold on to her, and as she pulled away, he ripped it off and exposed her face.

They stared at each other for a split second before she sprinted toward the window, but the darn cat was underfoot, and she tripped, grabbing on to the desk chair for balance. Its wheels slid across the carpet guard, and she dropped hard to her knees, grunting in pain. Then she heard the click of the safety on a gun.

She inhaled a sharp breath, muscles tight. Oh god, she was going to die.

"Stand up," Bertrand said in a steely voice.

Sable rose slowly from the floor, hands shaking as she lifted them above her head. She scanned the desk and saw a paperweight, an in/out box, folders filled with papers, a computer, and a pen holder.

"Turn around, slowly."

Mind racing to figure out an escape plan, Sable did as he instructed.

"How did you get in here?"

Instead of answering, she flung the folder of papers at his face, at the same time stepping to one side. Bertrand fired off a wild shot and swatted at the pages.

Sable dashed for the balcony door. He fired another round, and she winced, twisting away from the spray of bursting glass.

She grabbed the railing and sailed over with the grace of a ballerina, suspended by both hands before she dropped to the balcony on the floor below. She did another hop over that railing and dropped to the grass, rolling to soften the fall.

Another shot, and Sable gasped, a lump of fear flying into her throat. The floor of the cement balcony above broke apart into chunks that rained debris on her head. She couldn't risk the next shot hitting her.

She sped away, Bertrand yelling at her in the darkness. He fired two more shots, one of them whizzing close to her ear. In all the years she'd been a thief, she'd never been in a situation where she had been shot at.

The heavy Bible bounced against her back, but she didn't slow down. She didn't look back.

Only a matter of time before more security guards came. She sprinted toward the wall and scaled it quickly. At the top, she glanced back and saw two men barreling toward her from the back of the house. They yelled at her, but she dropped to the other side.

Sable ran fast, heart thumping, stomach painfully tight with fear. She started the night happy this was her last job.

It was almost her last job for a wholly different reason.

2

Hunter strolled down the street at night, nodding at a couple hugged up and giggling as they passed by him.

This was his first time in Paris, but he'd been to France multiple times, preferring the southern region where the Mediterranean Sea lapped at the shores and a temperate climate beckoned all year round.

When he'd received the assignment to hand deliver important documents to a government official, he'd gladly accepted and then stayed a few extra days not only to enjoy the city but do some research on a personal project. He opted to stay in Saint-Germain-des-Prés, a neighborhood in the sixth arrondissement, known for its antique shops, clothing stores, and an upscale department store, Le Bon Marché—the oldest and longest running department store in the world.

Saint-Germain was also famous for its literary and artistic history. Staying here—where artists, poets, and writers once lived in the 19th and 20th centuries—made him feel closer to his true nature. A nature he'd only recently discovered.

Searching for his past, he learned his mother—a woman

he'd never known because he grew up in foster care after his father passed—had been a writer. That bit of information made him feel closer to her, though he harbored resentment at her abandonment.

Hands tucked into his pants and shoulders hunched against the spring chill, he strolled down a side street to the apartment building. Of course, while here, he'd partake of Parisian pleasures. A smile touched his face at the memory of time spent between the sheets with a woman he met at a club the night before. Brigitte. Their hook up had been casual and fun, the way he preferred his relationships. With promises to meet up again, they parted ways about thirty minutes before, when he took the subway back to his part of town.

His French language skills weren't the best, but he'd learned enough to introduce himself to women. A few smiles and the translation app on his phone did the rest of the work. Besides, once they were horizontal, words were no longer needed.

Hunter opened the outer door of the building. A stairwell ran through its middle, with apartments on each side. He climbed the flight of stairs to the one-bedroom apartment on the second floor.

The apartment used to belong to his friend, Hossam's parents. They recently returned to Morocco after years of serving in the French government. Hossam owned his own place in another part of the city and planned to rent this one to visitors looking for an authentic Parisian experience. For the time being, because of their friendship, Hunter stayed for free.

The location was perfect but so was the apartment. White walls allowed natural light to brighten the space during the day, as well as bring attention to the details in the historic building's interior. A crystal chandelier hung from the ceiling, above a parquet floor with a herringbone design, and in true Parisian fashion, the decor included a mix of contemporary and antique furnishings.

A gilded mirror hung above the fireplace in the living room, and additional mirrors in the bedroom and bathroom gave the illusion of a larger space. High ceilings with equally high windows that swung outward made it easy to climb outside onto the small balcony, where an iron balustrade allowed for an unobstructed view of the street below.

After a quick shower to slough off the sweat and sex of the night, Hunter tugged on a pair of boxer briefs and strolled into the kitchen. He didn't turn on a single light. He preferred the peaceful quiet of the dark, and with the curtains open on the large windows, enough light came thru from other buildings and street lamps that he could see clearly enough.

Standing in front of the refrigerator, he saw only fruit and leftover pizza from dinner. He shook his head, disgusted. He was in Paris—where good food was meant to be savored—yet eating as if he were at his place back in the States. The fully stocked apartment contained all the utensils, pans, and equipment needed to prepare meals, so he didn't have an excuse for being so lax. Tonight, he was stuck with cold pizza, but tomorrow he'd run to the market and buy food for a day or two.

He placed the two slices on a plate and opened a bottle of beer. As he lifted it to his mouth, a noise in the living room caught his attention. The front door had opened. He cocked his head and listened and heard quiet movement.

Slowly, Hunter set the bottle on the counter and crept to the wall nearest the door. Back to the wall, he inched closer to the open doorway and peered into the other room.

A small figure in a gray hoodie, black pants, and a backpack over one shoulder stood in the middle of the living room, as if listening. A woman or a small man.

The person then moved in a stealthy manner and placed

the backpack on the sofa. Definitely a woman. Her movements and the shape of her legs in the skin-tight pants gave her away.

When she turned in his direction, he swiftly shifted left and stood still, hoping she hadn't seen him. After a few seconds, he peered out again. She went in the direction of the bedroom, very quiet.

What the hell?

Hunter's eyes narrowed.

He slipped out of the kitchen and speed-walked toward the intruder, hoping to catch her by surprise. She must have sensed his presence, however, because she looked over her shoulder. That's when he pounced and grabbed her arms. She released a squeak of surprise but quickly recovered, adeptly twisting one arm out of his grasp and launching a fist at his throat.

He caught the blow and twisted her around, clamping his arms around her in a bear hug. She flung her feet up on the wall and pushed off. Hunter stumbled and his back hit the other wall, but he didn't let go. They tousled, soft gasps bursting from her lips as she tried to dislodge herself, but his hold only tightened. Hunter forced the woman's cheek and body into the wall, and she whimpered in pain. Yanking an arm behind her back, he pulled up, and she let out a sharp cry.

A wave of guilt washed over him. He didn't want to hurt her, but she'd broken into *his* apartment and could possibly mean him harm.

"Stop fighting me," he commanded.

He didn't know if she spoke English, but the word "stop" was almost universally understood.

"*Putain! Laisses-moi, connard!*" she yelled.

French it is, then. Based on his limited use of the language, Hunter understood those words were not a friendly greeting.

"Listen to me, I need you to stop fighting me," he grated, struggling to hold but not hurt her.

"*Fermes ta gueule!*" she screamed, a quiver of frustration in her voice. She stamped one foot.

Her actions were completely useless. He held one arm behind her back and the other arm into the wall. She was practically immobile and not strong enough to slip from the hold.

He couldn't help but notice the floral scent of her skin underneath a spicier musk, as if she'd been running or exercising. He shook his head, annoyed he noticed.

"If you don't stop fighting me, I'm going to break your arm," he said.

She yelled at him some more in French, and he yanked her other arm behind her back, holding both with one hand. She whimpered, and then he landed a quick chop to the carotid artery in her neck. She immediately slumped against the wall.

Feisty little thing, Hunter thought. She could have seriously hurt him if she had landed that throat punch.

He swooped the unconscious woman into his arms and placed her on the sofa. After a rapid change into joggers and a T-shirt, he pulled duct tape from a drawer and taped her upright to one of the wood chairs in the kitchen. He bound her legs to the feet and her torso to the back. Then he used butcher twine to tie her wrists together behind her.

Hunter flipped on the overhead light and pushed back the hood of the hoodie to reveal hair styled into thick cornrows. With a finger under her pointy chin, he tilted up the woman's lolled head.

A jolt of awareness charged through him.

Attractive. Makeup-free, with nutmeg-brown skin, curvaceous lips, and thick eyelashes curled at the ends. His loins stirred at his immediate attraction to her, but then he remembered this woman had broken into his apartment. No telling what she was capable of.

Time to find out exactly who she was.

He retrieved the backpack from the living room and

rummaged through the contents. No I.D., but he did find a thick old book. He placed it on the table. The first five pages were blank, and he flipped through the others. He couldn't read a word of it. Looked like old Latin, maybe? Huh.

He also uncovered a crowbar, a lock-picking kit, a drill, and a can of spray paint. Interesting.

He pulled a stack of cash from the front pocket and glanced at the unconscious woman. Clearly a criminal. She picked the wrong place to break into tonight.

Hunter retrieved his beer and pizza and took a seat in front of her. He ate the late-night meal while waiting for her to wake up.

3

able stared at the stranger. Helpless. Angry.

Her self-defense training hadn't worked against him.

Who was he and what was he doing here? This apartment should be empty. Hossam told her his parents had left the country, and he hadn't rented it yet. She should have known something was off when she didn't find the spare key he said he kept above the door. The missing key didn't keep her out, of course, but had she known someone occupied the apartment, she would never have entered.

Now she was stuck, taped to a chair with her hands tied behind her back with a complicated knot, forcing her arms tightly together. Sable wiggled in the chair but could barely move. The bastard had done a good job.

He stood over her with crossed arms, wearing burgundy joggers and a plain gray T-shirt. At least he wore more clothes now, better than his half naked appearance when he attacked her. Tall, about 6'1, he seemed to fill the kitchen. His physique really made him appear overwhelming. She hated to admit it, but he had a great body. Broad shoulders and intimidating muscles traversed the length of his arms. The too-small T-shirt emphasized his massive biceps and stretched taut across his impressive chest. If he slapped an "S" on it, she'd have no problem believing he was from the planet Krypton.

He was attractive, though not necessarily the type to turn heads, with arresting gunmetal gray eyes and brown curly hair and skin significantly paler than hers. A mixed-race man whose lips and the sandy-colored tint of his skin suggested one of those races was Black.

"Who are you?" he asked.

Sable stared at him and refused to answer.

He repeated the question in French. "*Qui êtes-vous?*"

"I don't have to answer your questions," she replied in French. "Where is Hossam?"

His thick eyebrows sank lower over his eyes as he clearly tried to decipher the sentences. Then he held up a finger, as if to say *Wait a minute*, and disappeared from the kitchen.

As soon as he left, Sable struggled against the restraints, hoping to uncover a weakness she could exploit. Unfortunately, she remained good and properly stuck to the chair. She jerked against the tape again, gritting her teeth but unable to break free.

When she heard the stranger coming back, she stopped moving and sat very still, keeping the scowl on her face. A waste of time. He didn't seem the least bit intimidated, and why would he be? He'd easily subdued her and was built like an athlete.

He carried his phone with him now and spoke into it. "Hossam is out of the country. Who are you, and how do you know him?"

He turned the screen toward her so she could read the words translated into French.

Her lips tightened in a refusal to answer, and she jerked her bound hands. Whatever he'd tied her with cut into her wrists, and she groaned at the pain slicing through her flesh.

The stranger spoke into the app again. "You can't break free, so you might as well give up, or that twine will cut through your skin."

She ignored him and continued to struggle until she was out of breath. Then she yelled, "*Laisses-moi!*" Let me go!

"If you know Hossam, why did you break in here?" He showed her the screen.

Once again she didn't respond, glaring into his eyes, more upset at herself than him.

"So you're not going to answer any of my questions?" This time he didn't speak into the app. He spoke directly to her.

Sable didn't change the expression on her face.

His gaze dropped to the phone in his hand. "Fine. I'll call the police and let them figure this out."

"No!"

His eyes narrowed, and a slick smile crossed his lips. "Oh, so you understood that, huh?"

Sable bit her bottom lip, angry at her outburst. He'd tricked her.

The lift in the corner of his mouth sent unsettling warmth through her loins. *Oh good grief!* she thought, thoroughly disgusted by her attraction to this stranger.

He gazed down at her with a speculative expression. "Are you in trouble?" Forehead wrinkled and worry in his eyes, he actually appeared concerned.

"Please let me go. I needed a place to stay, that's all. I knew Hossam owned this apartment, and that's why I came here." She didn't know where she would go when she left, but she needed to rest and figure out her next steps.

His eyebrows shot upward in surprise. "You're American?"

Sable nodded. "Yes."

"Why did you pretend you couldn't understand me?"

"Because I don't know you. This apartment was supposed to be empty, and I needed a place to crash for the night. Obviously, spending the night is out of the question because you're here."

He sat down and stared at her for a moment. Her gaze didn't waver.

"What's all this?" He waved at the contents of her backpack on the rectangular table. "Is this why you need a place to stay?"

Sable hesitated. She didn't want to answer, but maybe if she provided a little information, he'd let her go. "Yes," she answered reluctantly.

"You're a thief."

Sable tilted her head higher. "Those are my things."

"Yeah, right."

"I don't have to explain myself to you!" she snapped.

"Actually, you do." He leaned forward on his arms.

Her nose picked up the scent of cucumber-mint, and her nostrils quivered. His closeness disturbed her, and she tried in vain to edge backward, farther away from him.

He continued talking. "First of all, you're in the wrong. You broke into Hossam's apartment. One call to the police, and you'll be in handcuffs, so spare me the bad girl act. Second, wherever this loot came from, the owner has more than likely put in a call to the police to report their missing cash. You're in a lot of trouble."

Their gazes locked in a battle of wills. Finally, Sable said, "I'm not telling you anything until you untie me."

"You're not in a position to make demands."

"It's not a demand, but I have made an observation. Yes, I broke into Hossam's apartment, but the average person would have called the police. You didn't. Instead, you tied me up and proceeded to question me. Your actions tell me everything I need to know. You have no intention of calling the police. Besides, how do you think Hossam would react when he finds out you accused his friend of breaking and entering and got her locked up?"

"It's not an accusation. You did break into the apartment."

"Nonetheless, he and I are friends. Do you want to explain to him why I'm sitting in a jail cell?"

He smiled, which made him appear more attractive, and her insides clenched. His firm jawline was sprinkled with hair, and those lips... *whew*. If they'd met under different circumstances, she might have jumped at the chance to kiss him and do much more.

"I'll untie you, but only if you tell me everything."

"Why?"

"Because I'm curious, and whatever trouble you're in, maybe I can help you," he said.

"Who says I'm in trouble?"

"You're obviously in trouble because you broke in to what you *thought* was an empty apartment."

His sharp deductive skills annoyed her. "I don't know how well you know Hossam, but if there's anyone capable of helping me out of a tight spot, it's him, and he's not here."

He crossed his arms over his chest. "I'm also very capable."

The cocky way he spoke the words made Sable really study him. Who had she stumbled on to? Was he in the same line of work as Hossam? She couldn't be sure. She didn't know this man and didn't know if she could trust him.

"Untie me, and I'll tell you everything," she promised.

He didn't move right away, as if he didn't quite believe her. She held his gaze, though she'd lied through her teeth.

"Let's start with names," the stranger said, standing as he spoke. He pulled a knife from a kitchen drawer and walked behind her.

Though she didn't expect him to harm her, her shoulders tensed and lifted up to her ears.

"Relax," he said, cutting the twine. "I'm Hunter."

Hands freed, Sable rubbed the red lines that encircled her wrists where the twine cut into her skin.

"My name is Sable." Almost immediately, she wished she'd given her fake name.

Oh well. From here on out, she'd tell him only what she wanted him to know, and then she'd leave the apartment. She'd sleep in her car if necessary. Her most important concern was taking the Bible to her contact and having him authenticate it.

Then she was getting the hell out of France.

4

Hunter didn't trust Sable, but for now he'd listen to her story. She sucked down a bottle of water as his foot bounced impatiently, waiting for her to give him the details.

She sighed gratefully and set the empty bottle on the table. "Thank you."

Her low, sexy voice made a prickle dance through the dark blond hairs on his arms. He couldn't stop staring at her. She was a stunning woman, even with her simple braided hairstyle. Close-set hazel eyes gave her face a dramatic, sultry look. Her narrow nose upturned at the end over plump lips made for kissing—and sucking dick.

"The cash is mine," she said. "I wanted to stay at Hossam's because I work with an antique dealer near here, in Saint-Germain. I occasionally travel around France to help him purchase objects, and on a scouting trip at a flea market outside the city, I found this Gutenberg and bought it." She pointed at the book on the table.

"Why is that book so special?"

"It's a Bible, printed in the fourteen hundreds. As soon as I hear from the dealer I know, we'll set up a time to meet, and he can authenticate the Bible. Then I get paid."

Her story didn't ring completely true, but he didn't disclose his skepticism. "You said you needed help."

"Yes." Her eyes dipped lower for a second. "Some men saw me buy the Bible and followed me."

Liar, liar, he thought.

"Followed you?" Hunter repeated.

"The antiques business can be cutthroat. They want the Bible because they believe it's valuable."

"*Believe*?" He latched on to the uncertainty in the word.

She shifted and appeared uncomfortable. "I believed it was valuable, but now I'm not sure. I don't think it's a real Gutenberg."

"Why not?"

Sable shook her head and smoothed a hand over the leather cover. She had long fingers with neatly trimmed nails.

She opened the book and fanned the pages with her thumb. "I've had time to take a good look at it and have doubts. The paper doesn't feel right." She closed the book, her disappointment palpable.

"You didn't notice the difference at the flea market?"

"No," she replied, voice clipped.

He studied her in silence. "You went to the flea market *today* in a cat suit and hoodie?"

She pulled the zipper of the hoodie all the way to her throat. "I like to be comfortable."

He pointed to her lock-picking kit and the drill. "Are these typical tools for bargain hunting at flea markets?"

"I'm like a Girl Scout. I'm prepared for anything."

Hunter tapped his finger on top of the table. "Why don't I believe you?"

"I don't know. You have issues, I guess." She kept her voice steady.

"So, you're going to your friend to show him the Bible you bought?"

She nodded. "He can authenticate it."

"How much is it worth if it's real?"

Hesitant, she watched him closely. "A lot."

"If I wanted to do something to you, I would have already done it," Hunter said.

"Doesn't mean you can't change your mind."

"You know I can Google it and find out?"

She sighed. "If the Bible is real, it's worth fifteen million."

He whistled in surprise and glanced at the hardcover book. "For that thing?"

She gave him a patronizing smile. "That *thing* as you call it, if real, is extremely valuable because of the history behind its production. Only one hundred and eighty Bibles were printed in 1455 in Germany by Johannes Gutenberg. They were the first books printed on a new press he invented that revolutionized the dissemination of information.

"There are forty-nine Bibles left in the world, and this might be one of them. A complete Gutenberg is two volumes and worth as much as *thirty-five million dollars*. This is a complete first volume, unlike others which are only parts of the Bible because collectors have torn out pages and sold them individually. But... like I said, I don't believe this is the real deal." She frowned.

"What happens if it's not the real deal?"

Her expression fell, along with her shoulders. "It means I wasted my time."

He suspected a deeper reason for her distress, much more than simply wasted time purchasing a fake object. She didn't seem inclined to share any more information, so he didn't push.

Hunter ran a hand over the Bible. For her sake, he hoped it was legit.

"So, you were trying to hide out in Hossam's apartment

because men followed you from the flea market, because they think you have an authentic Gutenberg Bible. Did I get that right?"

Sable nodded. "I'm staying at a hotel, but I came here instead because it's closer to the dealer's shop. I figured I could stay the night and meet up with him first thing in the morning. I made sure I wasn't followed." She swallowed, and stark fear filtered into her eyes, forcing him to sit up at attention. "I know Hossam is out of town, but he leaves a key above the doorway. It wasn't there. That's why I broke in."

"How did you get here?"

"I drove. I have a rental."

Hunter remained silent for a moment and then asked, "When are you going to the shop to have your friend take a look at the Bible?"

"I'm waiting to get a response to the text I sent earlier. As soon as he gives the okay, I'll go to the shop. Hopefully, in the morning."

"I'm coming with you."

Her eyes widened. "What for?"

"Because there are people out there looking for you, and for fifteen million dollars, I suspect they're capable of anything."

"You're trying to scare me."

"You're already scared."

She didn't argue but shook her head. "I don't need an escort."

"These men could be dangerous. If they are, you're going to need more than an antique dealer to help you."

"Are you my bodyguard now?"

"Something like that."

She eyed him with suspicion.

"I don't want anything from you," Hunter assured her.

"You're doing this out of the goodness of your heart? If you really believe these men are dangerous and could possibly harm me, aren't you risking your safety?" She smirked and arched an eyebrow as if she'd caught him in a lie.

He smirked right back. "Trust me. They're the ones risking their safety."

Her eyes narrowed. "Who are you?"

"Never mind that, but know I can handle myself."

"CIA?" she guessed.

"Again, I can handle myself." He stood. "You don't have to leave. You can stay the night."

She watched him suspiciously and then put the Bible, the cash, and the tools in the backpack. "I don't trust you. Thanks, but no thanks."

She walked out of the kitchen and headed toward the door.

"You're heading out there, into the unknown."

She swung around to face him. "I'll be fine. I've been doing this a while."

"Antiquing?" he mocked.

"Yes," she said tightly, flashing a fake smile.

"Something tells me you've never experienced a situation like this before, where men followed you from the flea market." Her gaze dropped to the floor, confirming his suspicions. "You can stay here, rest for the night, and then go to the shop in the morning."

"You still haven't told me what's in it for you. Why are you helping me?"

"You're a friend of Hossam's, and I'm a Good Samaritan," he said.

He could see the wheels turning in her head. The distrust, which was understandable. If indeed the Bible was worth as much as she hoped, then it made sense she'd be suspicious of his motives.

"I *am* tired," she said in a low voice.

"I'm sure. Must be draining doing all that... antiquing in the middle of the night."

She glared at him, and he couldn't hide his amusement. He laughed. She was cute. A cute little liar. But she was a friend of Hossam's and needed help. That part wasn't a lie because he'd seen the fear in her eyes.

"You can have the bedroom. I'll sleep on the sofa."

"You don't have to do that."

"I'm a gentleman. I insist."

He went down the hallway and heard her quiet steps behind him. She remained outside the door as he bundled clothes and other items he'd need for the night and morning in his arms.

She eyed him warily from the hallway.

"Are you always this standoffish?" Hunter asked as he approached.

"I don't know you," Sable pointed out. She remained guarded, body stiff.

He stopped in front of her, peering down into her upturned face. Definitely a nice mouth. Under different circumstances, he'd be making a pass at her.

"If it makes you more comfortable, lock the door."

"I plan to." Sable slowly slid past him, dragging her back along the wall to the door.

Hunter laughed softly. "Yeah, that'll keep me out."

She paused and stared at him.

"Do whatever you need to do to make yourself feel comfortable. In the morning, we'll eat breakfast and then go see your friend. Don't steal anything." Hunter headed back toward the living room.

"Ha, ha."

"Good night," he said over his shoulder.

"Good night."

Sable slammed the door, and he heard the lock engage.

He snickered with a shake of his head. She had no idea who

he was or what he was capable of. A paltry lock couldn't keep him out if he wanted inside that bedroom.

Hunter dropped the pillow and linens on the sofa, then hauled off his T-shirt and joggers. He preferred to sleep in as little clothes as possible.

Dressed only in boxer briefs, he went into the kitchen and grabbed a protein bar. As he peeled back the wrapper, he sauntered into the living room and over to one of the large windows. Bracing an arm on the frame, his eyes scoured the side street below where a smattering of pedestrians marched along the cobblestones.

Sable was right to question him. No, he wasn't CIA. He was much more dangerous than those guys, having been recruited into a secretive government agency called Plan B when only a teen. Which never would have happened if he hadn't committed a violent crime—one he didn't regret—at the age of fourteen.

He'd been raised in foster care from a baby. Deemed a problem with anger issues because he spoke his mind and didn't allow adults to get away with shit, he'd been shuffled in and out of too many homes to count.

When he learned his new foster parents lived in an upper middle class neighborhood, he'd been ecstatic. Another kid lived there, a thirteen-year-old girl, and they each had their own room. He'd always had to share and considered his own room a luxury, and he lucked out in such a nice house with generous and friendly foster parents—Mr. and Mrs. Henley.

He'd heard stories of great foster parents and finally had two of his own. Pillars of the community, the man worked as an attorney and his wife as a doctor. Hunter vowed to be on his best behavior so he'd never have to leave.

Within weeks, he'd sensed something was wrong but couldn't figure out what. One fateful night after returning from the kitchen with a midnight snack of Oreos and potato chips, he heard low murmurs and crying coming his foster sister's bedroom. With the door cracked, he silently entered.

At first, his young mind couldn't comprehend what he saw. He stared in disbelief at Mr. Henley on top of his foster sister. The adult didn't know Hunter had entered the room, too busy whispering who knows what as he committed an unspeakable crime.

His sister's quiet sobs wrenched at Hunter's heart. He barely remembered what happened next. He only knew he became engulfed in fury, sick and tired of bigger people hurting smaller people. Sick and tired of adults who didn't do what they should. Protect. Teach. Care for kids.

He grabbed the chair from the desk in the corner and marched toward the bed.

Mr. Henley finally heard him and looked up in shock. "H-Hunter, you should be asleep," he sputtered.

Hunter swung the chair with all his might and knocked the man off the bed. High on adrenaline, he kept hitting him. The chair broke apart, and he didn't stop, using a broken piece to inflict more damage. When he did stop, Mr. Henley lay half dead on the carpet. He died on the way to the hospital.

Later, when the police were hauling Hunter away, Mrs. Henley kept yelling at Hunter, calling *him* a monster. Not her husband, who assaulted a child placed in his care. It dawned on him then that she'd known all along.

A representative of Plan B came to see him in juvenile detention, but they deemed him too young to start training. The charges were dropped and his records sealed, but at sixteen they returned to get him. At eighteen, he killed for a second time, his first as an assassin for the organization.

Hunter stepped away from the window. Crushing up the empty protein bar wrapper, he tossed it on the coffee table. He spread the sheet on the sofa and tufted the pillow before dropping onto his back on the soft cushions.

He'd help Sable, make sure she delivered the Bible to her contact—more than likely a fence for stolen goods. Then he'd return to concentrating on the reason he remained in Paris days after completing the delivery for his agency.

To find the object that was a connection to his past.

5

S able dropped her bag on the bench at the foot of the bed and tried not to think about Hunter's laughter—a warm, deep sound that filled his throat. Though his laughter was appealing, she hated that he had laughed *at* her. And she hated the way he made her feel. All jittery and tingly.

What the heck was wrong with her? She was practically breathless over a man she didn't know. A man who'd taped her to a chair, for goodness' sake!

"You're behaving like a crazy woman," she chastised herself, looking around.

The imposing four-poster queen bed was softened by white sheets and a striped quilt in baby blue, green, and white. Similar to other furniture in the house, the frame was made of heavy, dark wood with a traditional headboard. There were two windows, stark white walls like the rest of the house, and a heavy-looking dresser.

Despite the locked door, she felt oddly exposed and ill at ease. Maybe she was overreacting, but she needed to reduce her anxiousness. Sure, Hunter was a friend of Hossam's and was being nice to her, but she couldn't be too careful. She took a few minutes to drag the dresser across the room, huffing and puffing under the exertion of the arduous task until she finally positioned it in front of the door.

She sat on the edge of the bed and removed her phone from the backpack. She left her charger back at the hotel, but it was at fifty percent, which would last until morning. She checked her messages. Nothing from Michel yet. At this hour of the night, he might not see the message she sent earlier, but she wanted him to know she was back in the city and ready to meet up.

As if she conjured him with her thoughts, the phone rang and Michel's name popped up on the screen.

She answered in French. "Michel, thank goodness!"

"Hello, Sable, what happened?" Concern coated his voice.

"I got caught," she replied.

"What!"

"I have the Bible, but I barely escaped with my life."

"Tell me everything," Michel said.

She gave him the short version, including the mad rush from the countryside into Paris and Hossam's apartment.

Michel swore softly. "I'm so glad you're okay."

"The problem is, I don't know if the Bible is real."

"What do you mean?"

"It's off, but I'm not the professional. You are. How soon can I come by the shop tomorrow?"

"Sable, I'm not in Paris."

"Why not?" He knew she was taking the Gutenberg tonight and was annoyed he wouldn't be able to meet her right away.

"My absence couldn't be helped. The nurse called. My mother isn't doing well, and they couldn't calm her. I'll be in Normandy for another day. She should be fine after that, and then I'll return to Paris."

Sable felt guilty for her selfish thoughts. Michel's mother was under the care of a private nurse and sometimes became agitated. Whenever that happened, he made the drive to Normandy to calm her.

"I understand. Of course you need to spend time with your mother."

"I shouldn't be here past tomorrow, I promise. Then I'll give you a call or send a text, we can meet, and I'll take a look at the Bible. But my source was confident Moreau possessed the authentic version."

"That's why I want you to look at it. I could be wrong. I hope I'm wrong."

"And you're safe? Where you are?"

"Yes."

"Who do you think was murdered?"

"I don't know, but his face is vaguely familiar to me. I'm hoping I'll remember who he is."

"Someone famous?"

"I have no idea. Hell, could be he simply favors someone I've seen before. Anyway, I called the police. I did my part, and now it's up to them."

"I'm glad you're safe. I'll give you a call maybe tomorrow evening so we can set a time to meet."

"Sounds good. Take care." Sable hung up the phone.

She'd completed other jobs for Michel in the past, and over the past few years, he'd become a dear friend, checking in on a regular basis and offering advice about the antique industry. She met him through a mutual friend, also a thief, who suggested her for her first Parisian job with Michel because of her ability to speak French. The easy theft involved lifting a painting at a small museum that refused to return the family heirloom to a Jewish family, the rightful owners.

In the United States, she worked at an antique shop that sold high-end pieces and collectibles of historical significance. She started out as a cashier, worked her way up to assistant antique dealer, but knew that's as far as she'd go in the family-owned establishment, especially since she had a GED and no post-secondary education. Though she'd picked up a lot at the shop, she'd learned more about the industry from Michel. His wealth of knowledge was enormous.

Elbows to knees, she buried her face in her hands and sighed. Man, she really needed him now. What a mess. The two men she trusted were out of town at the same time, and she was stuck with Superman out there.

Speaking of which...

Sable lifted her head and eyed the dresser. Slowly, she rose from the bed and went to stand in front of it. She couldn't deny being curious about Hunter.

One by one she eased open the drawers. The bottom ones were empty, but the top two contained folded clothes—shirts and underwear mostly. She fingered his cotton boxer briefs, and at the thought of the stretchy material taut around his hips and butt, she blushed.

Hurriedly, she shoved her fingers between and under the folded clothes, searching for hidden objects but finding nothing.

She went to the closet, the entire time her ears primed to pick up the sound of movement through the thick walls, but all she heard was silence. A twinge of guilt pricked at her chest. Well, he'd warned her not to steal but didn't say anything about snooping.

Sable continued to dig through his belongings. A pair of shiny black leather shoes sat in the bottom of the closet. She recognized quality Italian craftsmanship when she saw it. She also found long-sleeved shirts, jackets and ties, and casual items. Most of his clothes were dressy, which meant he was a man who liked to look good. With his physique, she imagined he wore the hell out of a suit.

One eyebrow arched at the Prada label in one of the jackets. *Excuse me*, she thought. Could CIA agents afford Prada suits?

He didn't spare any expense in an effort to look good. They shared that trait in common. After living in poverty for years, she liked dressing up and didn't blink when splurging on quality items.

"What do we have here...?" Sable muttered, lowering to her haunches to examine an aluminum-finish makeup case in the bottom of the closet.

Locked.

No problem. She retrieved her lock-picking kit and promptly opened the case. Searching the interior, she lifted up the trays, surprised to find not only makeup and brushes, but silicone noses, colored contacts, and fake facial hair.

Huh. What did this mean?

There was more to Hossam's friend than met the eye, that's for sure. Hossam refused to give her details about his clandestine work. He'd never actually admitted he was a spy, but she was certain that he was. Was Hunter a spy?

Sable snapped the case closed and winced at the unintended loud pop. No chance Hunter heard her, but she paused anyway and listened for him at the door. When only silenced greeted her, she locked the case and placed it in the same spot where she'd found it.

She stripped down to her panties and climbed under the cool covers. Outside, the streets of Paris remained busy with people going to and fro—pedestrians and drivers alike. Somewhere out there, men were searching for her, and much as she hated to admit it, Hunter was right. She was scared.

At least one of the men knew what she looked like— Bertrand—and she worried they might be able to find her. That's why she truly hoped the Gutenberg was real. Then she could collect her finder's fee and be on her way. She wouldn't even wait until the funds were deposited into her account this time. As soon as Michel confirmed it was real, she was catching the next flight out of the country.

The total finder's fee was fifteen percent, but after Michel took his five for sending her the lead, she pocketed ten. In this case, the missing Bible would bring in a cool $1.5 million—her largest payday yet.

She only hoped she was wrong, and the Bible was legit, but she seriously had her doubts. Her area was history, but Michel was a certified document examiner. He'd know for sure.

Despite her concerns, she retained a small bit of optimism the Bible was a real Gutenberg. Because if it were fake, she'd been shot at for an inauthentic object. Not to mention, Moreau would have known the Bible was fake, which didn't make sense.

Why would he have the Bible locked in the safe if he knew it was fake?

6

The next morning, Hunter went to the market nearby and picked up groceries. He called through the closed bedroom door and let Sable know he was making eggs, bacon, and pancakes if she wanted any, to which she said yes.

In the middle of preparing breakfast, his phone rang. He recognized the number right away and smiled as he answered.

"Hello, Alissa."

"You lucky bastard."

At the lilt of her familiar Caribbean twang, he belted out a hearty chuckle. "Don't be mad at me because I speak a little French." He sprinkled salt over the cooking eggs.

"Your language skills are basic at best."

"Basic is better than your French skills, which are nonexistent."

"I know a few words," Alissa grumbled, and he could almost see the pout on her face.

"Not enough to get you an assignment in France, my friend," he said.

His assignment had been one of the easiest since joining

The Cordoba Agency. He'd arrived in Paris and delivered sensitive documents to a government agent. In exchange, the agency received payment for their work.

Hunter settled the phone between his ear and shoulder. "How's your latest assignment going?" he asked.

Their entire organization consisted of some of the most elite agents in the world, but they all understood the risks they took each time they went on assignment, no matter how minor the task. Anything could happen, and worrying about the people who'd become family to him was par for the course.

"Tonight's my last night," Alissa answered.

She was on security detail, one of several bodyguards for the teenage daughters of a billionaire visiting their father from overseas. The girls had been there for a couple of weeks and were flying back to their country tomorrow.

"What's next?" Hunter asked.

"If Cruz doesn't have another assignment for me, I might go home for a week or so." Home for her was St. Thomas, U.S. Virgin Islands.

"Well, you haven't been home in a while, so I know you'll be glad to go back, even if it's only for a week."

At the sound of movement in the doorway, he glanced over his shoulder. Sable walked in looking the same—a gray hoodie over a black catsuit, sneakers, and her hair in cornrows—yet more gorgeous in the morning light.

Damn.

"You still there?" Alissa asked.

"Yeah, I'm here." Hunter mentally shook off his stupor. He couldn't recall the last time he'd been struck dumb by a woman, but there was a first time for everything.

"I invited you to St. Thomas. One day you have to visit, and I'll show you around."

"Definitely."

A slight pause. "So, when are you going to see Hossam?"

"Whenever he gets back. You have a message for him?"

"No. Just curious." She tried to sound nonchalant.

"Uh-huh."

"I don't like your tone," Alissa said. "I better get some sleep. Lucky for me, the girls don't get out of bed until noon most days."

"Okay. Sure you don't have a message for me to relay?"

"Bye, Hunter."

He laughed. "Chat with you later." He disconnected the call. "Hope you're hungry."

"I am," Sable said. "Um, hope you don't mind. I got some clean towels and used your soap to wash up."

"No, I don't mind. I should have offered last night."

Wondering if she'd gone commando under her skintight clothes, his scalp heated as he worked with the spatula.

"Can I help?" Sable asked.

"You can pour the orange juice. I'm almost finished."

"I smell coffee," she said.

"Over there." Hunter pointed to the counter and watched as she went to pour herself a cup.

A few minutes later, he placed the food on the table, and they sat down to eat. He cut into the fluffy pancakes, smothered with melted butter and syrup.

Sable eyed him as she chewed. "Why are you being so nice to me?"

"Told you, I'm a Good Samaritan," Hunter replied around a mouthful of food.

"A Good Samaritan willing to risk his safety for no compensation is rare," she said.

"Would you rather I not come with you?"

Taking a sip of orange juice, she seemed to mull the question for a while. Then her gaze skimmed over his forearms and biceps under his shirt. "No, I think it's a good idea if you come with me. Then we go our separate ways."

"Fine by me." Hunter sipped his coffee. "What time are we meeting your friend?"

"Actually, we're not. He's out of town and won't be back until tomorrow."

"Then why don't we get your stuff from the hotel, and you can stay here tonight again?"

"I don't want to intrude," she said.

"No intrusion. You need a place to stay until your friend is available tomorrow, and as you pointed out, staying in this apartment is closer to the shop. We'll get your things, and you can stay one more night."

A faint smile touched her lips. "You really are a Good Samaritan."

"I try," Hunter said, sipping coffee and letting his eyes idle on her.

"Okay, I'll take you up on your offer."

"We'll leave after breakfast," he said.

They finished the meal and deposited the dishes in the sink.

"You should leave your backpack here. Take only a little cash and hide the bag in the back of the closet."

She nodded and didn't give him the usual sass.

As they headed out the door, Hunter extended his hand for the keys. "I'll drive."

Sable walked ahead of him. "I don't think so. It's my car. I'll drive. Plus, I know where I'm going."

"Standoffish and stubborn," Hunter muttered.

"The perfect combination," Sable quipped.

Her white, four-door Peugeot was parked a couple blocks away. Hunter's eyes swept the area and so did hers, but no one approached them. They climbed in the vehicle, and Sable set off for the hotel.

Upon arrival, she parked on a side street, and once again Hunter paid attention to their surroundings outside the boutique hotel. In his line of work, he constantly took stock of his environment. He paid attention to the cars parked nearby, pedestrians walking on the sidewalks, and guests entering and exiting the hotel. Inside, he made the same quick assessments, taking note of the customers lounging in the small lobby, employees helping check people in, and the location of exit doors.

He was not prepared, however, for the elevator. The small space barely fit the two of them. He'd never thought of his soap as sexy before, but cucumber-mint mixed with Sable's natural feminine scent in the confined space was torture. He'd slept with plenty of women—all over the world, different sizes, shapes, and colors. None of them ever made him do what he was doing now—stuff one hand in his pants pocket to keep from reaching for her and hemming her up in the corner of the elevator.

When the doors opened on the fourth floor, Hunter breathed a silent sigh of relief and rolled the tension out of his neck. One would think he hadn't had sex as recently as the night before. He might need to text Brigitte for another hookup this evening.

He and Sable walked to the end of the corridor, and Sable let them inside the tiny room, with only a twin bed and otherwise sparsely furnished. Nothing extravagant, but comfortable and clean.

"I'll pack up my toiletries," she said.

She disappeared in the bathroom, and Hunter strode to the window and looked out. Nothing out of the ordinary, only a few cars parked on the street. A couple of black ones were empty but inside a brown Toyota Yaris a hefty-looking man sat in the driver's seat, reading a paper as he munched on an apple.

Hunter pulled a granola bar from his pocket and peeled back the wrapper. He took a large bite and chewed.

His phone rang, and he answered immediately.

"Hunter! Glad I caught you." Hossam's voice came down the line. He'd lived in France half his life but continued to speak with the accent of his native Morocco. "I received an urgent voicemail from a friend, Sable Devereaux. She said she was on her way to my parents' place, and—"

"We met. She stayed at the apartment with me last night, and we're at her hotel getting her luggage right now."

Hossam blew a gust of air from his mouth in relief. "Thank goodness. When I was able to check my messages, I called her back but couldn't catch her."

"On the ride over she told me she turned off her phone to save the charge."

"Is she all right? She didn't sound good to me but didn't go into detail over the phone."

Hunter dropped his voice and peered over his shoulder at the ajar bathroom door. "She's fine, but I think she's in big trouble and doesn't want to say. When are you coming back to Paris?"

"If all goes well, I'll be there in a couple days."

Hossam was on an assignment. He used to work for a special unit of Direction Générale De La Sécurité Extérieure or DGSE, the French equivalent of the CIA. Now he worked as an independent contractor. Like Hunter, his specialty was wet work, but whereas Hunter was a sharpshooter, Hossam mastered the art of making his kills look like accidents or suicides.

Years ago, when he worked for DGSE, they met on a mission in North Africa—a joint task force between France and the United States to root out members of a terrorist cell hiding in Morocco. At the time, Hunter worked at Plan B.

The clandestine U.S. government organization had been charged with taking out domestic and international threats to the United States. When the organization was officially dismantled, the company he worked for, The Cordoba Agency, contracted to handle those types of missions going forward, on an as needed basis. At any time, the President could call on them, but if caught, the executive branch would deny knowledge of their involvement.

Not exactly the best circumstances. Yet, despite years of working behind the scenes to ensure the safety of the country's millions of citizens—and doing so without accolades—it was the only kind of work that sparked excitement in Hunter's blood.

He gave his friend a quick rundown of what occurred and their plans to meet with Sable's antique dealer friend the next day.

Hossam swore under his breath. "That's odd," he said.

"Very."

Sable came out of the bathroom with her toiletry bag, and Hunter covered the phone. "This is Hossam," he said.

"Hossam?" Her hazel eyes turned bright with excitement. At her expression, an unexpected surge of jealousy punched him in the chest.

Shit. Where did that come from? Hossam was his friend, and Sable—hell, she didn't mean anything to him. He barely knew her.

"Listen, I don't know what's going on, but nothing can happen to Sable," Hossam said.

"Nothing will," Hunter said in a neutral voice.

Sable popped open her suitcase on the bed and started rounding up stray items from the room—shoes, her charger, etc.

"I need to tell you something. Is she close by?"

"Yeah," Hunter said, settling on the windowsill.

"Between you and me, Sable's a thief," Hossam said.

"No kidding. I figured that part out," Hunter murmured.

"She's no ordinary thief. Simply put, she takes from the bad guys and gives to the good guys. Based on the message she left me and what you've said, I have a feeling she might be in over her head this time. I need you to keep her safe until I can get there."

"This is new information," Hunter murmured, keeping his voice low.

"It's complicated, but that's what she does. You know something about that, don't you?"

Hunter did. Their line of work required them to be comfortable doing bad things for good reasons. They lived by a certain code, but the average person's conscience couldn't tolerate the tightrope of gray lines they walked across during many of their missions.

"I do," he admitted.

"Take care of her, Hunter, until I get there. I'll do my best to arrive soon."

Hunter wondered about the nature of the relationship between Hossam and Sable. Was there something deeper than friendship between them?

"Let me talk to her for a minute," Hossam said.

"Sure. Hold on." He pushed off the window and walked over to Sable. "Hossam wants to talk to you," he said, extending the phone.

Once again, her face broke into a happy smile. "Hello?"

Yet again, the uncharacteristic surge of jealousy came out of nowhere and surprised Hunter.

He tightened his lips, making a valiant effort to force thoughts of envy from his mind.

7

The entire time Sable talked to Hossam, Hunter's gaze burned her skin and put her on edge. She avoided looking at him to ward off the intensity of his eyes—the intensity of what she *felt*.

He seemed to strip her bare with his penetrating stare, but right now he appeared displeased, practically glaring as she talked to their mutual friend.

As she finished packing, she wanted to tell Hossam about the murder but decided to wait until she saw him in person. The story had not appeared in a single news outlet. Since Mr. Moreau was a famous businessman, there were probably lawyers and publicists in involved. By the time Hossam arrived, the story should break, and she'd be able to explain the details from her point of view.

After she hung up, Hunter took the phone. "What did he say?" he asked.

She and Hossam had carried on the conversation in French.

"He told me to trust you and said I'd be safe with you until he can return to Paris."

"So you trust me now?"

"Hossam would not have told me to trust you if I shouldn't. He's vouched for you, and that's good enough for me."

Hunter nodded, and a moment of understanding emerged between them. Trust was paramount, but guilt niggled at the base of her spine. She hadn't been completely honest with Hunter yet, but she would be. She only met him yesterday, and she'd exercised caution in the information she divulged. When Hossam arrived, she'd tell them both everything.

Sable gathered up the rest of her belongings and put them in her rolling suitcase. With one last look around the room, she made sure she left nothing behind.

"I've got it," Hunter said, taking the handle on the suitcase.

His fingers brushed hers and scalded her skin. Sable snatched away her hand. She took two steps in reverse to widen the distance between them, and her back hit the wall.

He raised one eyebrow and then, ever so slowly, edged closer. He crowded her, looking down from his superior height, head cocked to the side. "You know I don't bite, right?"

His gray eyes suggested different. He looked like the kind of man who assaulted a woman with rough hand strokes and deep kisses and nips to her lips—and she'd love every second of it.

Before she could respond, Hunter took the rolling suitcase and exited the room. Sable closed her eyes for a few seconds and then followed.

After checking out, they climbed into her car for the ride back to the apartment and drove along the Paris streets without speaking for several minutes.

"How do you know Hossam?" Sable asked, breaking the silence in the car.

"We worked together years ago on a project."

"What kind of project?"

Instead of answering, he arched an eyebrow.

Sable sighed. "Let me guess. It's a secret. Are you still doing the same type of work?"

"No. I work for a security and investigative firm headquartered in Atlanta. The Cordoba Agency," he replied.

"You're a bodyguard?" No wonder Hossam told her to trust him.

"Yes, that's one of the services we provide."

She glanced at Hunter. He looked like a machine. He had ripped forearms and sat with his legs wide and one hand resting on his left thigh, muscles prominent beneath the worn denim. The white Henley made his skin appear paler, the sleeves shoved halfway up his forearms to reveal light-colored hairs reaching to his wrist.

He hadn't shaved this morning, so faint stubble continued to darken his jawline, giving him a slightly unkempt look that was endearing and sexy. She thought about kissing his cheek and what those coarse hairs would feel like burning her skin, her sensitive breasts as he kissed his way down—

Hunter swung his head in her direction, and her eyes darted to the road ahead. Mortified, she flexed her fingers on the steering wheel. He didn't know what she was thinking, but her little fantasy sent the heat of her embarrassment through her chest.

After a few minutes, Hunter said, "I'm about to tell you something, but I don't want you to panic."

She glanced sideways at him. "*Okay.*"

"I think we're being followed. Describe the men who followed you from the flea market."

Anxiety tightened her shoulders. "One of them was large, brawny, and had a full beard. I didn't get a good look at the others. What makes you think we're being followed?" Her eyes jumped to the side-view and rearview mirrors, searching for the culprit.

"Any of them chubby-looking?"

"Not that I recall."

"You see the brown Toyota Yaris two cars back, behind the gray Renault?"

Sable nodded, her heart going *thump, thump, thump* in her chest.

"I saw the same car parked outside the hotel, and now it's behind us."

Oh shit. Had they found her? "You're sure? What should I do? Should I try to outrun them?"

Hunter spoke in a soothing voice. "No need to do anything so drastic. Let's make sure we're actually being followed."

"But you said we're being followed!"

"I said I *think* we are, but I want to make sure. If we try to outrun him in traffic, we risk hurting ourselves and others. No point in taking that kind of chance unless we're certain we're being followed."

"And how in the world do we find out? Should I stop the car and go up to his window and say, excuse me sir, are you following us?"

Sarcasm was her coping mechanism to keep from panicking. She woke up twice last night, sweating as the nightmare at Moreau's estate replayed in her mind. Watching someone get murdered was traumatizing on its own, but running for her life while gunshots blasted at her in the night was an altogether more terrifying experience, forcing her to consider her own mortality and the choices she'd made over the years.

"What did Hossam tell you about me?" Hunter asked in a low voice.

"What do you mean?" Her eyes left the road for a moment to look at him.

"He told you to trust me, didn't he?"

She focused on the red car in front of her. "Yes."

"Good. Keep that in mind. The first thing I want you to do is calm down. Take a deep breath. You don't want to panic because when you panic you make mistakes. Okay?"

"Okay." He was right. She'd been in precarious situations before and staying calm and keeping a clear head had kept her safe. She inhaled and exhaled several deep breaths.

"Now, drive normally, but I want you to make four right turns. Not suddenly, but drive as if you're on your way to a specific destination."

Sable glanced at him. "Four right turns? Why?"

"Because four right turns or four left turns is essentially a circle. If the Toyota remains behind us the entire time, then we know we're being followed."

"Wow, makes perfect sense." She looked at him in wonder, but he only smiled.

Driving at a normal speed, Sable took the first right. The Renault went straight, but the brown Toyota also turned right.

Her abs tightened, and her fingers gripped the steering wheel. "He's still behind us," she whispered.

Hunter's eyes focused on the sideview mirror beside him. "I see. Make the next right up here, where the blue car is turning."

Sable turned, and seconds later, the brown car did the same. Her palms started sweating, and she recalled the overwhelming fear that gripped her when Moreau's man discovered her behind the drapes. Her heart beat faster as she recalled her race to the stone wall and the sound of bullets exploding in the night as they tried to end her life.

Despite Hunter sitting beside her, his confidence, and Hossam's confidence in his abilities, the sharp talons of fear gripped her.

"Take a right after the hotel up ahead," Hunter said.

Sable turned the wheel, following the line of traffic onto the next street.

She lifted her gaze to the rearview mirror, but the brown car was nowhere in sight. She briefly closed her eyes, almost collapsing in the seat.

"It's gone." Hunter spoke with finality.

She nodded at him, grateful. "Yes." She laughed, relieving the tension in the car and in her body.

"You okay?" Hunter's squeezed her knee.

His touched lasted only seconds to provide comfort, but the world stopped, and everything went fuzzy. Heat soared up her thigh, and her beating heart stammered in her chest.

Their eyes met, and the emotional strain of the past few minutes tightened under a different type of pressure.

"I... yes." Sable forced her eyes to the road ahead.

Hunter cleared his throat and straightened in the seat. "Okay, let's go back to the apartment," he said.

8

Sable changed into jeans and a long-sleeved shirt and felt more like herself after being forced to wear the catsuit and hoodie for way too long. She kept her hair in cornrows because it was easier, but smoothed her edges now she had her hair supplies. She then applied tinted lip gloss and eye makeup to boost her appearance.

She found Hunter in the kitchen, chopping garlic while browning chicken in a pan and paused in the doorway to study him. She could still feel his warm hand on her knee.

Watching him work, she had the distinct impression he was polished on the surface but sensed an underlying wildness, a sense of danger. The kind of man she liked. The kind of man she should stay away from. The kind of man to fuck you so good, within hours your head would be a tangled mess of wild hair and kinky roots.

She drew a sharp breath, hating the direction of her thoughts.

"Can I give you a hand?" she asked, walking into the kitchen.

His gaze lingered on her. Once again, his probing stare

made her feel naked under his perusal. The way he looked at her as if he craved her was disturbing, to say the least, but also exciting. His eyes dipped to her lips, and though he didn't say a word, she knew he liked what he saw in her moderately altered appearance.

"How good are you at chopping?" he asked.

"Excellent. What are we making?" She went to stand beside him.

"A quick chicken cacciatore."

"Whoa, I'm eating good tonight. Where did you learn to cook?" Sable washed her hands.

"I learned to fend for myself pretty early in life."

Interesting.

She wanted to learn more while at the same time needing to keep her distance.

A man like Hunter screamed that he offered everything she tried to avoid—things she no longer wanted in her life. Passion. Fireworks. The excitement of risky behavior. She was no longer an immature teenager making bad decisions. Older and more mature, she knew better—right?

"What do you plan to do with your finder's fee once you collect it?" he asked.

"Why do you ask?"

"I sensed that losing this fee was more important than simply being a waste of time."

Sable worked on peeling an onion while she talked. "You're good, and you're correct. I want to open my own antique shop."

He glanced at her. "Really?"

She nodded. "It's been a dream of mine for a while, and regular conversations with Michel have been helpful. By the way, I heard from him. He opens the shop at eight but told me to come at ten. The shop tends to be busy when he first opens, but there'll be less foot traffic by then."

"When he gives you the good news, where do you plan to open the shop?"

Sable gave a little laugh. "You sound confident about the authenticity of the Bible."

He turned the browning chicken thighs with tongs. "You have to put positive thoughts into the universe for positive things to happen."

"Oh, really? I didn't take you for the kind to believe in something like that."

"You mean all that woo-woo stuff, as people say?" His smile was sexy, endearing. "I believe in the power of positive thinking. It's gotten me through some rough periods in life when things weren't going the way I wanted them to. Keeping my hopes up made me behave in a different way, which ultimately benefited me."

"I need to be more like you," Sable admitted, scraping half a chopped onion to the side of the cutting board. "Life hasn't always been easy for me, so getting the finder's fee is important."

"You're opening your shop in the States?"

"Yes. I'm an assistant antique dealer at a family-owned store in Nashville, Tennessee, but I've learned way more from Michel."

"How often do you come to France?"

"Not often," she replied, purposely vague.

"What about relationships?" Hunter set down the tongs and gave her his undivided attention.

"What about them?" Sable blinked back tears from the onions and rushed through chopping the second half.

"No ring, so I assume you're not married, and I'm wondering if you have a man waiting for you in Tennessee."

"Do you have a woman waiting for *you*?"

"I asked you first."

Sable scraped the onions into a bowl and placed a small plate over them. "I have a friend."

"Friend with benefits?"

"Something like that," she muttered with reluctance. She had needs, after all, and she and her "friend" had established a mutually beneficial understanding. No fuss, no muss.

"So it's not serious?" Hunter prodded.

Setting down the knife, Sable said, "You're not my type." What a big fat lie.

He let out a short laugh. "Whoa, where did that come from? And what type am I?"

"Definitely not the type to settle down with one woman. You're a player."

"Oh, come on." He popped a raw baby carrot in his mouth.

Resting a fist on her hip, Sable lanced him with a look. "How long have you been in Paris?"

Chewing, he shrugged. "Five days."

"How many women have you slept with since you've been here?"

He stopped chewing as if caught off guard. "That's irrelevant."

"That many?"

Sable hauled the bowl of mushrooms toward her, suddenly annoyed.

"So you have a problem with players?"

"I have a problem with community peen."

She'd learned her lesson a long time ago to stay away from his type. She'd grown up fast, and messing around with someone who didn't do commitment had landed her in more trouble than she cared to reflect on at the moment.

"Hold on, I do *not* have community peen."

"International peen?" she asked sweetly with a fake smile.

"I'm a nice guy. Friendly."

"Sure. Women just fall on your friendly dick all the time, don't they?"

Sable didn't want to think about why she was giving him a hard time or the jealousy that made her want to stab the cutting board. How many women had he slept with in Paris in a mere five days? Hell, she'd been with him almost a full day already, so it was really only four days!

"A second ago you told me you have a fuck buddy."

"Yes, but he's not slanging his thing all over Nashville."

"That's what you think."

She shot him a glare.

"I thought you and I could hang out after your big payday tomorrow, but I guess not."

"I don't need any more friends to distract me. I have responsibilities to worry about," she muttered.

"Like what?"

Sable slammed down the knife and looked at Hunter. "Like my daughter, Avril, who's in college."

Taken aback, his eyebrows snapped lower over his eyes. "You have a kid in college?"

"Yes, what of it?"

"How old are you?"

She'd been in this situation before, but after a while, she decided not to be ashamed and not let the judgment of others force her to lie and hide the truth. She loved her daughter with her whole being and didn't regret having her. Her only regret was that she hadn't been able to provide her the life she deserved.

"I'm thirty-three. I had my daughter at fifteen. She's thriving and happy, and I want her to stay that way."

"Where does she go to school?"

She saw curiosity in his eyes but not judgment. Yet, there was always judgment below the surface, which made her confrontational and put her guard up.

"Gallaudet University in DC. It's a school for the deaf. This is her first year, but she loves her classes, and she's made a lot of friends."

"For the deaf. So..."

"Yes, she's deaf."

"You use sign language?"

"Yes."

"How many languages do you speak?" he asked, sounding impressed.

"Only three," Sable said nonchalantly. Calmer, she went back to chopping the mushrooms. "English, French, and American Sign Language. I speak French because of my father. He was from Guadeloupe."

Hunter returned to tending the chicken. "Where are your parents?"

"Why so many questions?"

"Excuse me a sec."

He reached into a cabinet above her, and she held her breath. They didn't touch, but he emitted a warmth—an energy—which bathed her entire body in heat.

Hunter placed a large can of crushed tomatoes on the counter. "I'm curious about you, and besides, what else is there to do except talk? Do you really want to work in total silence?"

Shaken yet again by her reaction to him, Sable kept chopping for a bit. She wasn't sure she wanted to share more of her personal life with Hunter, but she'd been closed off for so long, it was almost a relief to open up to someone. Yet opening up meant being vulnerable, and she didn't know if she wanted to go there. Especially because of her outrageous attraction to him.

"My parents are dead," she answered reluctantly. "They died when Avril was a year old. Ever since then, it's been me and her."

"I'm sorry," Hunter said.

Sable shrugged. "I was sixteen but determined to be a good parent after my bad example growing up. My parents weren't terrible people, just indifferent. They shouldn't have become parents. *C'est la vie.*" She shrugged again as if it didn't matter, but she'd carried the pain of their neglect for years. She didn't hate them. She'd simply been immensely disappointed and determined to smother her daughter with the love, affection, and attention she never received. "They were musicians and used to leave me alone a lot. I was screwed up for a while, acting wild, the usual nonsense. Dumb and immature, but having to take care of Avril made me grow up fast."

Everything she did was to provide a better life for herself and her daughter.

"What about you?" she asked.

"I don't know anything about my family." He turned off the rice in the pot. He no longer looked in her direction, and his short answer was a clear attempt to close her out.

"Nothing?" Sable asked, heart aching for him.

He dropped a pat of butter on the rice and stirred. He took so long to respond, at first she thought he would ignore her question. When he finally spoke, she didn't move a muscle, afraid the slightest movement might cause him to stop talking.

"I'm working on finding out more. My whole life I thought I'd been abandoned, but my history is a little more complicated than that. Through the agency I work for, I discovered my mother was French. She's dead now, but years ago she visited New York and met my father. They had an affair or some shit, I don't know. Anyway, she moved back to Paris and left me with him. He died, and with no immediate family available to take me in, I was put in foster care when I was less than a year old."

"How could they put you in the system when you had a mother? Did she know—"

He slammed the cover on the pot, and Sable jumped.

"I have no idea. She died a few years after my father, and she was a novelist. That's all I know for now."

From that moment on, their conversation steered clear of personal topics as they worked in the kitchen.

Sable wanted to pull him into a hug and chase away the hurt with soothing words and a back rub. She understood how he felt. She'd been there, struggling with resentment and anger coexisting with the love for her parents, but she'd had years to deal with her mixed emotions. His wounds were fresh and wide open, and only time would allow them to heal and close. The emotions haunting him would not disappear anytime soon.

Forty-five minutes later, they sat down to dinner. The tender chicken fell off the bone, its fragrant sauce perfumed with thyme and garlic. She gave him suggestions on places to visit in Paris before he returned to the U.S., and he made her gasp and laugh out loud with a couple of stories about hard-headed clients.

He recounted one story about a teenager who snuck out the window of her home to go clubbing and almost got implicated in a shooting at the same club. Then another about a celebrity client who insisted on driving himself to his mistress's home and ended up falling asleep at the wheel on the way back. He crashed through a fence into a neighbor's pool. Days later, his wife started divorce proceedings.

After they put away the dishes, Hunter did the same as the night before, removed his clothes, bedding, and a pillow from the bedroom. A few minutes later, Sable padded out to the living room.

She drank him in, lying on his back wearing only jeans and no shirt, head propped on the pillow as he scrolled through the news on his phone. Curly dark blond hair sprinkled his muscular chest and arrowed to the waistband of his jeans.

"You going to stand there all night, or do you have something to say?" he asked, gaze never leaving the phone.

Her cheeks burned. Folding her arms over her chest, Sable said, "I feel a little guilty about you having to sleep out here."

Hunter sat up and paused to let his heated gaze tour her body, lingering on her breasts and traveling to her hips. Fire blazed in her blood at the blatant male appreciation in his eyes.

"Don't. This sofa is comfortable." He gave the cushion a firm pat. "I've slept in worse conditions, believe me. Of course if you're really feeling guilty, we could share the bed. It's queen-size, so there's plenty of room."

"I don't think so."

"Why not? Don't trust yourself?"

His full lips twisted into one of those sexy smiles, and she knew she was in trouble when the apex of her thighs pulsed with warmth. She'd known Hunter a mere twenty-four hours, and in that short period, he'd become more attractive and more tempting.

"I don't trust *you*," she said pointedly.

His smirk suggested he sensed her internal conflict.

"Good night," she said.

"See you in the morning. If you change your mind, you know where to find me."

Sable marched away in a huff. Without looking, she knew his eyes followed her until she was out of sight down the hall.

9

H unter checked his watch while he drained the last of the coffee from his cup. "It's almost ten. We should get going."

Sable, seated at the table across from him, nodded and stood, and his eyes followed her lithe movements. She was toned, with defined muscles in her arms and legs. Since she didn't work in a field that necessarily required a lot of physical activity, he assumed she must work out often.

She appeared to be in a good mood today, perhaps optimistic about the visit to her friend. That's not why he couldn't take his eyes off her, though.

She'd released her hair from the cornrows. A crown of reddish brown hair, the color obvious now that she'd removed the braids, kissed her cheeks and cascaded past her shoulders in a wavy pattern. On one side, the shiny strands rested against the top of her breast, bringing attention to their fullness and forcing his abs to tighten in rampant awareness. No sit-ups for him later. He'd sat with his stomach tight all during breakfast.

She wore light makeup again, which brought attention to her lovely lips and made her close-set eyes appear sexier and more inviting. Marble print designer jeans fit her ass as tight as Cling Wrap, and a heather gray top fell off one shoulder, exposing the strap of her white bra. If he made it through the day without filling his hands with her bottom and kissing those sweet-looking lips of hers, he deserved a medal for restraint.

They left the apartment and walked down the stairs and into the street. Sable placed her sack in the back seat, and Hunter climbed in the passenger side.

"How far to your friend's place?" he asked.

"Ten minutes."

She pulled into traffic, and as she mentioned, they arrived at her friend's antique shop in a short time. Les Antiquités de Paris, the name of the shop, was on a street with other businesses, including restaurants, small cafés, furniture stores, and other antique shops.

"He hasn't opened yet," Hunter said, observing the vintage FERMÉ sign on the glass door as they waited for the light to change. He didn't see any activity inside.

"Strange," Sable murmured, frowning. "He should be there, and the shop should be open by now."

"Circle the block," Hunter said.

Her head swung in his direction. "What for?"

"Just do it." He kept his voice firm, brooking no argument.

She followed his directive and drove past the shop. Hunter's gaze swept the area, noting the parked vehicles and people sipping coffee as they ate at tables on the sidewalk outside the cafes.

"There's Michel's car," Sable said, pointing to a red vehicle.

"So why isn't the shop open?" Hunter asked.

Sable gnawed the corner of her lip.

"Is it normal for him not to open when he's there during normal business hours?"

"He could be getting coffee. Or maybe he changed his mind

and didn't open today, so he could catch up on work he missed while out of town." Sable glanced at Hunter, eyes hopeful.

He didn't respond. He didn't want to alarm her or dull her good mood, but the skin on the back of his neck tightened with unease.

"He said he'd be here. He wants to verify the Bible as much as I do," she added.

A couple of vehicles passed by, but nothing on the street gave Hunter cause for concern. No one sitting in their cars, and no vehicles seemed out of place.

"Circle around one more time," he said.

"Okay." Sable's voice sounded small, and her fingers tightened on the steering wheel. "You're making me nervous."

"Don't be nervous. I just think it's odd your friend said he'd open the shop, but we're here and it's closed."

After the second drive around the block, Sable parked a couple cars behind Michel's vehicle.

"What now?"

"Text him. Tell him you're here."

She did as he asked, thumbs traveling fast over the numbers. After five minutes, there was no reply.

"He should have responded by now," Sable whispered.

Hunter looked at her. "What do you want to do?"

She swallowed. "He knows I was coming today. Let's see if he's there."

They exited the vehicle, and Sable flung her sack over one shoulder. They jogged across the street and walked to the front door. They peered inside, but it was dark. Sable wiggled the knob. Locked.

"Maybe he's in the back," she said.

By the doleful expression in her eyes, he knew she was grasping at straws but determined to remain optimistic.

"Then let's go around back." Hunter shot a look over his

shoulder. Pedestrians walked by, but no one paid them any attention.

They passed between two buildings to the back. Hunter scoped out the area—quiet, with a few shops and green space with plenty of grass and the beginning bloom of flowers.

Sable knocked on the door and waited. "Come on Michel, where are you?" she muttered. She waited a few seconds and then said, "I'm going in."

She dropped to her haunches and, removing her tools from the backpack, proceeded to pick the lock. Hunter kept a look-out, and within seconds, the door was open. Damn, she was fast.

Sable moved to enter first, but Hunter held her back with a hand on her shoulder, and she stepped aside and let him cross the threshold. The scent of old leather and dust greeted his nostrils as he paused, listening, but didn't hear any activity. Was Michel here or not?

The space was stuffed to the brim with furniture and boxes stacked all over. Every visible shelf contained objects—from old cameras to silverware, books and propaganda posters, lamps and old metal lanterns. The items were all in varying stages of age. To the left, an open door led to a small bathroom.

Hunter crept through the store, and Sable followed close behind. A floorboard creaked underfoot and he stopped. Sable bounced into his back and paused. His ears didn't pick up any sounds except the distant noise of traffic in the street out front.

He resumed walking, passing through another small room stuffed with items in better condition and tagged with hand-written price tags. Cigar boxes, a chandelier, an old chest opened to show the contents inside. They approached another room. From this angle, it appeared to be an office, and from his line of sight, it was the last room before the sales floor out front.

Hunter entered, and his heart sank. The place was trashed, papers thrown everywhere, drawers yanked out of furniture and turned upside down, their contents strewn across the floor. But the disarray was nothing compared to the sight of the dead man.

Behind him, Sable gasped.

A blond, white male was taped to a chair, face drained of color and lips blue, garroted with piano wire. Blood dribbled from the wound and soaked his collar and the front of his beige shirt.

Sable slapped a hand over her mouth. "No. Michel." She turned her face away from the deadly scene.

Hunter squeezed her shoulders, and she suddenly pressed her face into his chest. His arms locked around her to offer comfort as she sobbed quietly into his chest.

When she finally pulled back, she angrily swiped at her tear-stained cheeks. "He didn't deserve this."

"Don't touch anything," Hunter said.

He stepped over a pile of books on the floor, inspecting the area as he walked behind the chair Michel was taped to.

"They tortured him," he said in a grim tone.

Circular burn marks dotted his exposed forearms, as if someone pressed the hot end of a cigarette into his skin multiple times. The sickening odor of burnt flesh lingered in the air.

"What were they looking for?" Sable asked, eyes wide as she scanned the room.

Hunter didn't answer, but his gaze dipped to the backpack on her shoulder.

Her eyes went wider. "You don't think...? His death might not be related!"

"There are very rarely coincidences."

"But I don't think the Bible is real."

"Either they came for the Bible, or your friend is involved in some shady dealings." Hunter brushed the back of his hand to the cup of coffee on the desk. Still warm. Whoever killed

Michel hadn't left that long ago and could still be in the area. Perhaps watching. "We need to get out of here."

"I can't leave him like that!"

"We'll call the police when we're safely out of here."

Hunter didn't wait for her to agree. He headed toward the back door. He knew Sable was following because he heard her shuffling feet and sniffling behind him.

On the way out, he wiped down the doorknob to remove their fingerprints and then walked briskly toward the main street.

They stopped on the sidewalk and waited for a black BMW sedan to amble by. Sable was quiet, eyes trained on the ground, probably in shock after what she saw.

Hunter remained attuned to his surroundings and zeroed in on the car, senses on high alert. He'd noticed the same car passing by earlier. He might not have noticed them, except for the tinted windows. The vehicle moved slower than the others, as if the driver was lost or looking for something. Could be nothing, but its appearance twice within such a short window was at the very least an odd occurrence. As if they were circling the block, the same as he and Sable had done.

As the car passed, the driver—a Black man wearing sunglasses—turned his head to look at them. Dark tinted windows in the back hid a passenger in the back seat, but he had a clear view of the man next to the driver. Big, brawny, with a full beard. He matched the description of the man Sable said followed her.

Tension coiled in his spine. A dead antiques dealer and three men circling the area, one of them matching the description of someone who'd scared Sable. He didn't like this at all.

Hunter committed the license plate number to memory and grabbed Sable's arm. "Let's go."

She looked up in alarm as he dragged her down the sidewalk. "What's wrong? What's happening?"

"I think I saw your brawny, bearded friend."

"What?" she squeaked.

"Give me the keys. I'm driving."

They rushed across the road to the side street.

She removed the keys, but her hands were shaking so badly, they dropped to the ground. Hunter swiped them up before she could bend over to grab them. They walked toward the car, Sable going toward the passenger side and Hunter to the driver side.

He was about to shove the key into the door when the squeal of tires caught his attention.

The BMW barreled toward him. His body grew taut.

There was no way to outrun them in the narrow side street, and he didn't have enough time to get out of the way.

10

Sable watched in paralyzing horror at the collision about to take place, but right before the car hit his legs, Hunter hopped up and flung his body over the hood.

Sable staggered back, her scream mingled with the sound of crunching metal as the Beamer sideswiped her Peugeot. Hunter rolled over the side of the BMW, which kept moving and crashed into a Renault two car lengths down.

Hunter scrambled to his feet as if nothing happened, eyes trained on the BMW as he rolled his shoulders, as if to check if any bones were broken. She couldn't believe he was in one piece.

"Run!" he yelled.

They took off down the street, and the black car reversed toward them at breakneck speed.

Hunter ran over to Sable and grabbed her lower arm. They dashed across the main street, almost getting run over by a white van, whose driver leaned angrily on the horn and yelled out the window at them in French.

Hunter's long legs ate up the pavement as he dragged Sable

along. She did her best to keep up, but her shorter legs burned with the effort.

A loud bang cracked the air, and the window of a parked car shattered into pieces. Sable screamed and pedestrians ducked and scattered in different directions. Hunter dragged her behind a van delivering furniture to an antique shop a few doors down from Michel's store. The delivery men looked around wildly, and Hunter swept past them with Sable in tow.

A quick glance over her shoulder indicated the men in the sedan were hot on their tail, no longer in reverse, and gunning for them with a mangled front end and little regard for pedestrians and other cars.

Bertrand, the bearded man from the night at Moreau's estate, was leaning out the window with a gun. When another shot shattered the morning air and sent more pedestrians hollering and running for cover, Sable pumped her legs faster.

She followed wherever Hunter led. Fear raced through her veins, forcing her heart to beat abnormally fast. She had no idea what Hunter's skill sets were, but he had an air about him, as if he'd done this before. He was controlled, with a quiet confidence that instilled trust in his ability to protect her.

They rushed toward an intersection, and their pursuers gunned the car engine. Sable's legs burned, but she ran hard to keep up with the man gripping her forearm.

At the intersection, Hunter barely paused, and they bolted across the street. Sable winced at the blare of angry car horns and the screech of tires as they dodged through traffic. Sweat dripped down her face, and the backpack with the heavy Bible bounced repeatedly against her hip.

They ran to a cafe and dashed past a few diners. Startled guests and wait staff looked up as they burst into the belly of the restaurant.

Chest heaving, Sable stayed close to Hunter as they rushed toward the kitchen.

"You can't go back there!" a waiter yelled.

They pushed through the swinging door. Cooks and waiters twisted stunned gazes in their direction. Hunter didn't stop moving. He shoved a waiter with a tray out of the way, and the man spun in a circle. The dishes he carried crashed to the tile floor.

Sable apologized profusely in French as they hurried toward the back door. No one tried to stop them, and they exited into a dead-end alley.

"Come on," Hunter said.

She was exhausted, but he wasn't slowing down. She was in good shape but didn't know how he managed to function at such a high level.

They raced toward the open end of the alleyway, but the Black driver from the BMW came tearing around the corner on foot. They skidded to a stop.

"Back! Go back!" Hunter blocked her with his body as a shot rang out.

Ducking, panting, screaming, Sable scrambled to the safety of the kitchen.

Inside, Hunter locked the door, and they ran back toward the front of the restaurant.

Through the large window with the name of the establishment and the day's specials scrawled across its surface, she observed the car at a standstill on the opposite side of the street.

"They're trying to box us in," Hunter said in a grim tone.

Oh shit, Sable thought.

"*Bonjour.* Would you like a table?" one of the waiters asked, his words pleasant but his lips held in a tight smile.

"*Non, merci.*" Sable turned to Hunter. "What do we do?" She expelled heavy breaths from her chest.

"Ask him if there's another way out of here, not through the back," Hunter replied.

"*Pardon, monsieur, on peut—*"

Hunter uttered a four letter word, and Sable turned in time to see the car come barreling toward them for a second time. Two diners on the outside screamed in panic and flung their bodies to either side of their table. The car barely missed them as it crashed through the chairs and tables, scattering utensils and shattering glasses and plates. The driver kept coming and smashed through the glass door and window of the cafe.

More screaming as terrified diners scrambled out of the way.

Hunter shoved Sable none too gently in front of him toward the staircase leading to the lower level where the bathroom was located—typical for many eating establishments in Paris.

Bullets splintered the ceiling and shattered the lighting fixtures. Women and men shrieked at the noise.

"Everybody, out!" one of the gunmen yelled in French.

She and Hunter scrambled down the narrow, winding staircase and into a dimly lit hallway. There was no way out. They were stuck.

Sable burst into the unisex bathroom, Hunter right behind her. The small room contained a urinal, sink, and a toilet inside a narrow stall.

She couldn't stop shaking. Twice in less than a week she was running for her life.

She spun to face him. "I don't want to die."

"You won't if you do what I say. Get in the stall and don't come out until I tell you."

"What are you going to do? They're going to kill us."

"Not if I can help it. I prefer to run to escape a dangerous situation. It increases the odds of survival. But we have nowhere to run now, so we have to attack. We'll take them by surprise."

"You're insane."

Her comment didn't faze him. "Get in there, now. We don't have much time before they come downstairs."

On unsteady legs, Sable went into the stall and pulled across the latch. She put her eye to the crack in the door and saw Hunter pull a black object from a holster on his ankle, and she heard a click. A switchblade. He held up the knife in a clenched fist and planted his back against the wall.

What did he think he was going to do with that thing? Those men had guns! They were going to die. She rested her forehead against the cool stall door. She didn't want to die in the basement bathroom of a Parisian cafe.

"*Sortez maintenant!*" one of the men outside yelled.

She lifted her head. "He's telling us to come out."

"Come out so you can kill us? No, thanks," Hunter called back. His body noticeably tightened. The muscles in his jawline and forearms became rigid.

The man laughed. "You are American. You are very brave. Or very stupid." He spoke with a British accent.

"Why don't you come in here and find out?"

Silence on the other side.

Sable remained unmoved, frozen, and her feet cemented to the floor. She didn't dare breathe as she awaited the next words or actions.

"We want the Bible, that's all," the man said.

"Why? We believe the Bible is fake. Why do you want it so bad?"

"We don't care what you think. It's ours. Your girlfriend took something that doesn't belong to her."

"Is that why you killed her friend at Les Antiquités de Paris?"

The man let out a dry laugh. "Give us the Bible, and we'll leave you alone."

"Somehow I doubt that, seeing as you have guns. If you just

wanted it, you could have asked nicely, and we would have turned it over."

"Somehow *I* doubt *that*," the Brit said. He tapped the door with what sounded like the muzzle of the gun. "Give us the Bible. Now." He didn't sound as amenable as he did before.

"Come and get it," Hunter said in a low, dangerous voice.

Ohmigod, ohmigod, ohmigod.

The door was kicked in, the frame splintering and pieces of wood shooting into the air.

A dark-haired man came charging through the door, his weapon stretched in front of him with locked arms. Hunter moved fast. He grabbed one of the man's wrists and shoved the gun away from him. Two shots blasted through the air and destroyed the mirror above the sink. Sable jumped and covered her ears from the explosive sound in the cramped space.

Hunter jabbed the knife into the man's armpit, and he howled. Hunter yanked out the knife and stabbed him in the torso two times in fast succession. As the Brit crumbled bleeding to the floor, Hunter snatched the gun from the dying man's fingers and cropped to one knee.

He blasted two shots through the open door.

A thud as a man Sable couldn't see dropped in the hall.

Kill shots.

But a third man was out there.

"*Putain!* Give us the fucking Bible!" he bellowed in accented English.

Bertrand. She recognized his voice from the other night and shivered in her tennis shoes.

Hunter didn't respond. He held the gun in both hands, unmoving on one knee, head bent and ear cocked as if listening. Sable watched in fascination.

He barely breathed. He'd easily killed two men, and there wasn't a scratch on him. Only blood splatter from the man lying on the floor.

He seemed calm and unbothered while she was screaming inside.

All of a sudden, Hunter flung his body through the open door and landed on his side. He pulled the trigger. One! Two! Three! Shots cracked in the air. One answering shot from the other man's gun splintered the wall above Hunter's shoulder.

Sable waited in the silence.

Another thud.

11

Hunter jumped to his feet and picked up his knife. He wiped off the blood and slid the blade back into the notch.

"You can come out now," he said. He sounded so normal.

Slowly, Sable exited the stall. Who was this man? Apparently someone capable of killing three men while trapped in the cramped basement of a Parisian cafe.

The stabbed brunette on the ground groaned.

Hunter aimed the gun and put a round in his temple, ending his misery. "I should keep this since this country's laws didn't allow me to bring a gun with me," he muttered.

Instead, he wiped his prints off the gun and placed it next to the dead man. Again, all very normal. Nothing out of the ordinary here!

He dug in the brunette's pockets.

"What are you looking for?" Sable asked.

She put a hand over her nose. She wanted out of there as quickly as possible. The nauseating odor of death and blood and the sharpness of gun smoke permeated the air. Suffocating.

Making it hard to breathe. She desperately needed to pull fresh air into her lungs.

"Checking for I.D." He came up empty.

Hunter stepped between the man's legs and into the hallway. She followed and watched him pat down the other men and rummage through their pockets. He pulled a wallet from Bertrand's pants.

"Let's go." He moved toward the narrow staircase, not bothering to check if she followed.

But of course she did. She looped her arm through the second strap of the backpack and secured it on her back, stepping over the dead bodies in the dim hallway. They stopped climbing at the third stair from the top. The restaurant was empty, but sirens sounded in the distance.

Hunter's eyes went to the sidewalk. "We can't go out the front."

Sable stood on her toes and followed his line of sight to the gathered crowd and people taking photos of the carnage caused by the BMW.

"We'll go through the kitchen," he added.

"What about my car?" Sable asked.

"Forget it."

Keeping low, they duck-walked around tables and overturned chairs, broken glass crunching under their feet on the way to the kitchen. After checking the alley, they slipped through the back door and trotted toward the street.

A police car whizzed by with lights flashing and siren blaring. Sable tensed, but walked calmly as if nothing was amiss. Other sirens drew closer.

As they walked, Hunter tugged off his blood splattered shirt, leaving a white T-shirt underneath. Drops of blood had soaked through, but their appearance was minor compared to his dress shirt. He crumbled the bloody top into a ball and tossed it in the trash, not once breaking stride.

"Where are we going?" Sable asked.

She hadn't fully processed what happened. After their ordeal, her knees were shaky, and she struggled to keep up.

"Back to Hossam's." Hunter glanced over his shoulder.

Sable did too but couldn't tell if anyone was following them.

He grabbed her arm, and she gasped.

Lowering his voice, he said, "You have some goddamn explaining to do. It's time you tell me the truth about that Bible."

Sable tugged away and expanded the distance between them as she walked. "I don't know what you mean. I did tell you the truth," she insisted, feet moving double time to match his long-legged walk.

"Your buddies back there specifically said they wanted the Bible. They didn't almost kill us because of a fake book. And since when do antique dealers have their throats sliced open with piano wire? The antiques business can't be that goddamn competitive. No way he's only an antique dealer. There's something going on here, and you owe me the truth."

"Michel was going to tell me if the Bible was real or not. That wasn't a lie."

Her stomach twisted with grief. Poor Michel was dead, killed in a savage murder that would probably give her nightmares tonight. What would happen to his mother without him?

Hunter didn't appear satisfied with the answer but kept a brisk pace down the sidewalk.

"I didn't lie about the Bible, but there is more I need to tell you. Can we talk about it when we get back to the apartment?" Sable asked.

He glared at her, then he took the stairs into the subway. All Sable could do was follow.

∾

Jean-Jacques Moreau sat at his desk at his company headquarters in La Défense, the business district a couple of miles outside Paris. The latest shipment was on the move. He watched on his computer from a secure app.

As the owner of multiple antique shops that delivered and picked up items around the country, he tracked all his trucks the same way but paid extra attention to the ones carrying the precious cargo from his Corsican partner.

He hadn't always been involved with drug traffickers, but he'd gotten himself into a financial jam years ago. For a long time, he'd made money buying and selling some of the most sought after antiques. Except they weren't authentic. He'd been mass producing fakes at his warehouse, treating the objects with specific techniques to make them appear old. Once discovered, he denied knowing anything about the fraud and paid his manager to take the fall and do the short jail time. Moreau also paid massive fines and suffered a devaluation of his inventory, which crippled his business.

Then five years ago, Elan Crimini approached him with the opportunity of a lifetime. The Corsican drug trafficker's family dominated a huge chunk of the drug trade in western Europe and Russia and needed a partner for their France operation. Ever since then, Moreau's life changed. He expanded his fleet of trucks and vans, and the money started rolling in.

While Europol concentrated its finite resources on surveilling the port of Antwerp—known for years as the cocaine capital of Europe—the Corsican gangs moved product almost undetected through the port of Marseille. The city struggled with gang violence, and the outcry for help had been fierce of late. The victims were getting younger—teenagers and most recently, a young girl of only nine.

The French government worked hard to stop the importation of drugs but struggled under the effort. The drugs were smuggled in a number of ways. Inside dolls, lining the interior of appliances, and stuffed into hollowed-out pineapples. Every now and again, officials uncovered a shipment, not even a tenth of what was imported on an annual basis. As long as the traffickers could bribe officials and dockworkers, the government would continue wasting their time, rolling a boulder uphill.

The intercom on his desk squawked.

"Mr. Moreau, I have a call for you. It's Philippe." His executive assistant's husky voice came through the speaker.

"Put him through."

"Hello, Mr. Moreau," Philippe said.

Philippe was his right-hand man—a personal assistant, a jack of all trades, a fixer—and the one person in his organization he trusted above all others.

"One of our friends in the police department contacted me and wanted you to know about a massacre over in the Saint-Germain neighborhood. Three men were killed in a Parisian cafe. He said—"

"What does that have to do with me?" Jean-Jacques asked impatiently, signing a document his executive assistant placed on his desk earlier.

"I was about to tell you, sir. Our friend recognized one of the men as Bertrand."

Jean-Jacques snatched up the receiver. "What did you say?"

"Bertrand was handling the situation—"

"I know what he was doing," Jean-Jacques hissed.

The last he spoke to Bertrand, he and the others dealt with the antiques dealer and found out the name of the woman who stole the Bible. He knew all the players in the antique business, and few of them were dumb enough to accept stolen goods. Through the process of elimination, they found Les Antiquités de Paris and pulled information from the owner about the theft of the Bible.

"Bertrand told me he took care of the antiques dealer. How did he end up dead?" Jean-Jacques asked.

"According to witnesses, there was a Black woman and a man who disappeared from the scene before the police arrived."

"A Black woman?" No way it could be the same woman they had been hunting for. "Are you telling me that woman and a friend killed the members of my personal security team?"

"I'm afraid so."

Absolutely incredible.

Jean-Jacques rubbed his brow. "This woman has caused me a lot of trouble. She not only stole a valuable object from me, she killed some of my best men, and got away. Again!"

There was silence as he considered next steps.

"I think it's time we go to our backup plan," he said.

"Are you sure, sir?"

"Yes, I'm sure!" he snarled. "Flush the bitch out."

"I'll start working on that right away."

"*Today*, Philippe."

"Yes, sir."

Jean-Jacques hung up and ran a tired hand down his face. There was no rest for the weary, but perhaps he could relieve the tension coursing through him.

He picked up the phone. "Lisa, get in here."

The door opened almost immediately, as if she'd been standing outside waiting for his call. A platinum blond, she wore her hair in a severe bob with bangs. Her blue eyes always carried enough heat to melt ice in a snowstorm.

Her red bodycon dress would raise eyebrows in a different office environment, but not a soul dared say a word to him, or her for that matter.

"Close the door."

The lock slid into place with the touch of her hand, and she crossed the room with a sexy stroll worthy of a Parisian catwalk.

"How may I serve you?"

The question immediately aroused him. She was a husky-voiced American he'd hired two years before. One of his better hires. The diamond tennis bracelet he gave her for Christmas sparkled on her wrist. He was certain she'd never taken it off during the past four months.

"I received some terrible news that's made me rather tense."

Her mouth fixed into a pretty red pout. "I'm sorry. I think I can help make you feel better."

Placing her hands on the armrests of the executive chair, she twisted him to face her. Then she lowered to her knees and dragged down the zipper over his growing bulge.

Another life-changing perk of his financial success was the number of women he had access to and how willing they were to do his bidding. Unlike his frigid wife, an ex-actress—also blond and American—who couldn't act her way out of a paper bag. She certainly did not *act* as if she enjoyed his company anymore.

One day he'd get rid of her. Until then, he received the relief he needed from other sources.

As Lisa's lips closed over his hardening erection, Jean-Jacques closed his eyes and let her mouth suck away the concerns of the day.

12

After exiting the subway station, Hunter and Sable took a circuitous route to the apartment to ensure they weren't being followed. Up and down streets, doubling back, and then taking yet another street.

Sable knew it was necessary to ensure they weren't being followed, but by the time they climbed the stairs and entered the apartment, she was exhausted and sore where the backpack with the heavy Bible had bounced against her hip bone as they ran from their pursuers.

Once inside, she blocked her cell number, dialed 112, and reported Michel's murder.

As soon as she hung up, Hunter walked into the living room and planted his feet apart in front of the fireplace.

"Talk." His teeth crunched into a red apple.

She had hoped to avoid this conversation in lieu of a warm shower to scrape the muck of sweat and death off her skin, but as she watched Hunter with his arms crossed over his chest, she realized her keen desire to clean up and refresh would have to wait. He looked resolute in his favorite pose, and though a coffee table separated them, his glowering no-more-bullshit stare intimidated her.

"You first," she said from the soft armchair.

He arched an eyebrow.

"You showed incredible skills out there. You know how to avoid getting hurt when someone tries to run you over, and you killed three men with guns while we were boxed in down in the basement."

"I told you, I work for a security and investigative firm called The Cordoba Agency. I've gone through years of training."

She didn't believe he'd given her the whole answer, but she wasn't exactly in a position to judge. "Your years of work included some incredible training." She challenged him with direct eye contact.

No response.

Men like Hunter had probably been trained to keep secrets while being tortured. Her death stare was laughable.

"At least tell me this, were you CIA before you started at your agency?" People in his line of work often came from military or intelligence backgrounds, which could be where his skill sets came from.

"No," he answered in a clipped voice.

"Care to share anything else?" she asked.

"No."

"Let me guess. If you told me, you'd have to kill me."

"More or less," Hunter said dryly.

He might be kidding, but after the display at the cafe, she couldn't be sure.

"Do you mind having a seat?"

"I'm good right where I am." He bit into the apple again.

Sable sighed in resignation. "Fine," she muttered. "I'll tell you everything, but you have to promise not to judge."

"You're asking an awful lot."

"It's necessary because of what I have to tell you."

"Did you kill anyone?"

"No."

He assessed her in silence. "Can't promise I won't judge, depending on what you have to say. Tell me what's going on."

Sable expelled a deep breath. "Do you know who Jean-Jacques Moreau is?" she asked.

Hunter shook his head. "Never heard of him."

"He's a businessman who got in trouble years ago when inspectors discovered he was creating fake antiques and selling them as authentic pieces. Well, he claimed he didn't know anything about the fakes and that his manager was the mastermind." She rolled her eyes. "His reputation took a hit, and he lost a lot of money. Since then, there have been rumors of him dabbling in other illegal activities, possibly transporting more than antiques."

"Drugs?" Hunter prompted.

Sable shrugged one shoulder. "Possibly. Can't say for sure because charges against him never stick. He has a lot of power and connections. One time he was questioned about a dinner he hosted at a local restaurant that included members of the Criminis, a drug-trafficking—among other things—mafia family from Corsica. He claimed they were antique lovers.

"I basically wanted to put a dent in his personal collection by taking the Bible, which rightfully belongs to someone else. It's been missing for years, and when we heard he had it, we wanted to get it back. The rightful owner couldn't convince the police to issue a warrant to search his home based on a simple accusation. Moreau being an upstanding citizen and all."

"His connections keep him out of trouble."

"Exactly."

Hunter lowered onto the chair across from her and put the apple on the table. Resting his elbows on his knees, he asked, "How did you find out about the Bible?"

"Michel. He really is an antiques dealer, but through his network, he finds out about objects of value that have ended up in the wrong hands, and people like me... procure them. Michel charges a finder's fee for returning the goods to the rightful owners, usually five to ten percent. Someone else was supposed to have this job, but when they couldn't do it, Michel asked me because I pulled other heists for him in the past. He trusted me and knew I could do it. This time, he negotiated a fifteen percent fee—five for him and ten for me. A huge payday considering the appraised value of the Bible, but the owner was desperate and excited because he never thought he'd see the Bible again."

"So you're a thief."

"I'm more than a thief," Sable said with indignation. True enough if she were caught, she'd go to jail, but she wasn't a mere criminal.

A smile of amusement lifted the corners of his lips. "Sure." Hunter sat back, his narrowed gray eyes studying her.

"I don't care what you think, Hunter, but I'm not a common criminal."

"What are you then?"

Sable straightened her shoulders. "I right wrongs by taking from the bad guys."

"A thief who steals from the bad guys." Interest sparked in his eyes, and oddly enough, she had the distinct impression this man not only understood, he was already aware of her profession. "So this Moreau guy, you took his Bible. How did he find out?"

"I got caught, and I saw something when I lifted the Bible from the safe in his home office." Hunter's eyebrows shot toward the ceiling. "Yes, I took the Bible from his home. I didn't buy it from a flea market, but you already figured that out. Anyway, I saw someone get murdered in his office, and Moreau was *right there*. One of his employees—the bearded guy—killed a man, and he was the one who discovered me after Moreau left the office. In the struggle, I lost my mask but managed to escape.

"I told Michel this was going to be my last job. My goal has always been to open my own antique shop, and I found a place in Nashville that's almost ten thousand square feet. Perfect location downtown. With Michel's mentorship and what I've learned from working at the antique shop in Tennessee, I could do it. But everything went wrong the other night."

She went into more details, including how she was discovered because of her allergy to cats. Hunter shook his head in disbelief.

"Once I got away, I called the police and left an anonymous tip about what I saw."

"But nothing happened."

She shook her head. "Nothing at all, and I've kept my eye on the news."

"So there's a dead body on Moreau's estate, or he's already dumped the body. Any idea who the murdered man is?"

"I know his face, but I can't remember where I know him from. Hopefully, it'll come to me at some point."

Hunter rubbed his temple. "Okay, let's forget about the murder for a minute. The first thing we need to do is figure out if this Bible is real because they really want it back. There must be a reason why."

"It's not real."

"How do you know?"

Sable removed the Bible from her bag and opened it on the coffee table. "Going to Michel was just a formality, trying to remain optimistic, but he taught me well. The one hundred and eighty Gutenberg Bibles I told you about? Most were printed on paper, but others on vellum. At that time, Gutenberg would have used calfskin to make the vellum. Vellum was more expensive, obviously, and as a writing surface more uneven."

"So your client's copy was printed on vellum," Hunter deduced.

"Yes. Vellum was sometimes damaged during the printing process. Those sections were sewn together and were detectable." She lifted a single page and rubbed it between her finger and thumb. "This is a well-done replica. A fake, like the fake antiques Moreau sold years ago. These pages are pure paper. No cracks anywhere, only smooth surface."

Hunter knelt in front of the table and ran a hand over the Latin words. His long fingers caressed the page, and Sable ignored the movement and thoughts of how those hands would feel caressing her skin in the same way.

"If this is a fake, why do they want it so bad?" Hunter asked.

"I don't know. It's not worth much."

He locked eyes with her.

"You have to be careful, Sable. You're a witness to a murder, committed under the instruction of a wealthy man who is possibly a criminal with ties to the government and mafia. His people know what you look like and found Michel's shop and you in under forty-eight hours. The people you're dealing with have lots of resources, and they don't call the police when they're robbed. As you saw today, they handle it themselves. I killed Moreau's witnesses, so all he probably knows, for now, is a man was with you and helped you kill them. But they're still looking for you."

13

After his chilling announcement, Sable rubbed her hands up and down her goose-pimpled arms and sank lower in the chair.

Hunter was right. She thought about Michel with his cut throat, and a shiver rattled through her. Lifting a hand to her own throat, she swallowed. She would have been killed today if not for Hunter.

"Whether legit or not, they want this book," Hunter continued. "We have to figure out why. You'll have to trust me, Sable. Do you trust me?"

She readily nodded. After today, she'd be a fool not to. He'd not only saved her, he'd risked his own safety to do so. "Yes."

"Good." Hunter rose to his feet and removed the wallet he'd lifted at the cafe. He shifted to sit on the sofa and flipped it open.

"Bertrand Matisse. Do you know this address?" He turned the wallet so Sable could see the contact information.

She nodded. "That's Moreau's address. Maybe Bertrand lived on site?"

"That would have made him a permanent, full-time

employee. Kind of unusual for the owner of an antiques company to need twenty-four-hour close protection service. Moreau is definitely up to no good."

Hunter removed colorful euros from the wallet and tossed them on the table. He sifted through a few credit cards and opened a folded piece of paper.

"What does this say?" he asked, handing it to Sable.

She glanced at the French words. "Nothing important. It's a shopping list."

Hunter tossed the wallet on the table in frustration. "I was hoping we'd find something to help us understand why they want the Bible so badly."

"What do we do now?" Sable asked.

"I'm going to run to the market to get more food. We skipped lunch, and I can't think on an empty stomach." Hunter pushed up from the sofa and picked up the apple.

"Buy wine. Plenty of it, please."

His mouth twisted into the semblance of a smile. "We'll figure this out, and you're going to be fine."

"I hope so." She desperately wanted to believe him.

For a moment, they looked into each other's eyes, and she longed to jump up and throw herself into the comfort of his arms the way she had at Michel's shop. She didn't, though, and the moment passed.

"I need to change out of these clothes, and then I'll leave."

"Okay."

Emptiness filled her as she watched Hunter walk toward the bedroom. He hadn't left yet, but the distance between them made her feel alone. Absolutely ridiculous, but she wanted him near. The world was safer, better with him near.

"You're losing it," she muttered.

She'd been on her own for years and didn't need anyone. Certainly not a man who was practically a stranger.

Sable flipped on the television and saw news coverage of

what happened at the cafe earlier. Footage showed officers milling around the scene and curious bystanders on the outside of the police tape.

She went to the kitchen and retrieved a bottle of water, all the while listening to the female reporter at the scene speculate about why the BMW crashed through the front of the cafe.

She returned to the living room and stood beside the sofa. Eye witness descriptions of Hunter were all over the place. They called him a white man, a light-skinned Black man, a mixed race man, an Arab man. The only consistent description was his height. When the newscaster at the desk talked about Sable, he referred to her as a short Black woman with a black backpack.

"I'm not *that* short," she mumbled, taking a sip of water.

Hunter came down the hall, changed into a long-sleeved shirt, jeans, and a baseball cap. She startled when she saw a mustache on his upper lip, and his gray eyes now brown.

"Don't act surprised. I know you were snooping in my shit," he said.

Her cheeks burned with guilt.

"I won't be long. Anything else you want besides plenty of wine?"

His soft smile warmed her heart. Her honesty had broken down a wall between them.

"Do you mind stopping at the bakery a few doors down and getting me some macaroons? I—"

She broke off and swiveled her head in the direction of the television, mouth falling open at what she saw.

The newscaster was talking about the murder at Moreau's estate, but that's not why her mouth fell open. In the upper right corner was a passport photo of her with the alias name she used—Veronica Shaw.

"Hunter," she whispered, staring at the television. Pressure built in her head.

"Holy shit." He came to stand beside her. "What are they saying?"

A video showed a masked intruder in Moreau's home office. He'd had a camera in his office the entire time! The video had been shortened, because the next frame showed her fighting Bertrand and the moment he pulled off her mask. The frame froze on her features.

Sable placed a hand to her nauseous stomach.

Two images flashed on the screen. One of a smiling Michel in front of his store, the other of the man she saw murdered at Moreau's estate.

Sable's hand shook as she pointed to the man on the right. "He was a member of the French Parliament. That's why I recognized him. His name is Richelieu—Senator Richelieu. But that's not the bad part." Sable gulped. "They're looking for his murderer, and according to Moreau's security, that person is me. Hunter, they're saying I'm wanted for the murder of both men. The senator *and* Michel."

14

A short video of the boutique hotel Sable checked out of flashed on the screen before returning to the reporters at their desk.

Hunter didn't understand what the reporters were saying, so Sable translated.

The man and woman speculated about her alleged murderous tendencies. They questioned who was this American woman, and how was she connected to the murder of the three men in the cafe? The lead detective refused to give any details, only speculating there could be links to organized crime. He ended by encouraging Veronica Shaw to turn herself in.

"How did they find me?" Sable whispered.

"They tortured your friend, Michel. He probably gave you up before they killed him. Lucky for you, he gave them your alias and not your real name."

"Oh my goodness." She staggered to the sofa and dropped onto the cushion, burying her head in her hands.

Hunter stooped in front of her. "Listen to me, we're going to get you out of this."

She lifted her head. "*How?*"

He couldn't stand how distraught she looked. "We'll find a way."

"From here on out, I'm stuck in this apartment, a prisoner because I'm wanted for two murders. And if they can pin the other three on me, they will. There's hardly any mention of you! My world is falling apart, and it's all because of that stupid book!"

Hunter grabbed her wrists. "Look at me, they're not going to get away with this. *I* won't let them get away with this."

She closed her eyes and noticeably relaxed, as if his words provided comfort. "You should go."

"I don't want to leave you."

"We have to eat, and I'm not leaving this apartment any time soon."

Hunter didn't want to go, but he stood. "I won't be long."

Sable nodded.

"Hey." He tilted up her face to his. "Trust me."

"I do," Sable said quietly.

On his way out the door, she called, "Don't forget the wine!"

Hunter first stopped at the butcher. As he waited for the meat to be wrapped, he considered the accusations against Sable. Moreau was using Michel and the senator's murders to smoke out Sable. That's the only thing that made sense. She would be their scapegoat for the death of the senator, and they'd use police resources to track her down. Because of his connections, Moreau probably stayed in contact with at least one person on the police force who'd keep him abreast of the case against her. If she made any accusations of her own, he'd already made a preemptive strike and discredited her.

Hunter shopped quickly, keeping the cap low on his head as he picked up supplies. CCTV wasn't as prevalent in Paris as in London and New York. The French preferred their privacy and made a greater fuss about the intrusion of cameras, but he couldn't risk being careless. Cameras were still everywhere, at ATMs, protecting storefronts, or in smartphones, all of which could be accessed by the government if necessary.

He returned to the apartment with two bottles of wine and enough food to last a couple of days.

Sable was in the same spot he left her in on the sofa, bare feet on the chair and hugging her knees. She looked defeated.

"You okay?"

"Yeah, I guess." She managed to smile.

Hunter went into the kitchen. He put away the groceries and folded the empty paper sacks, placing them under the sink with the others. He returned to the living room and sat in front of the table.

"I have a thought about the Bible. I think the reason Moreau wants the fake Gutenberg so bad is because he has something hidden inside it. It's the only thing that makes sense."

He picked up the Bible and turned it over and over in his hands, searching for something out of the ordinary. He then flipped through the sepia-colored pages while Sable looked on.

"There's nothing there," she said.

Hunter placed it on the table and opened it at the center. "There could be a hidden code in the words," he said, staring at the pages.

"But where? Do you speak Latin?"

"No."

He retrieved a letter opener from the desk in the corner and inserted it in the spine. He worked the spine loose, separating it from the pages and then peered into the empty space.

"Nothing," he said, disgusted. He'd hoped there might be a hidden slip of paper inserted in there.

"Then it must be in the words, like you said. I doubt Moreau speaks old Latin. Maybe the words are in French and sprinkled in between the Latin. We'll have to go through every page to check, though," Sable said.

A daunting task. There were hundreds of pages.

"We can't work on an empty stomach. We have hours of work ahead of us. I'll start dinner." Hunter stood.

"While you're cooking, I'll take a quick shower."

The innocently spoken words rested on the air between them for an awkward moment before Sable scurried toward the hall.

Hunter's gaze dropped to her firm butt in the tight, marble print jeans. He was glad she ditched the hoodie. The loose covering had hidden her shapely figure, and he much preferred the current view.

When she finished, she returned to the kitchen in another pair of designer jeans and a cotton blouse molded to her body. He averted his eyes from the protrusion of her hefty breasts and concentrated on cooking. They worked together the same as the night before, except less talking this time because of the much more somber mood.

The evening's menu consisted of grilled steak, roasted potato wedges, and a salad of Brussel sprouts topped with a simple dressing of balsamic vinegar, honey, and olive oil which Sable whipped up.

Seated across from her, Hunter smelled the fresh scent of what he assumed was lotion or body spray—something light and delicate—certainly more enticing than cucumber-mint. She'd pulled her hair on top of her head and allowed ringlets to tumble around her face.

Sable dipped a potato wedge in ketchup. "Either these are the best potato wedges I've ever tasted, or I'm hungrier than I thought."

"I'm going to take the compliment and believe my secret seasoning is what makes them so good."

"Oh really? What's your secret seasoning recipe?"

Her hazel eyes sparkled with humor, which he was glad to see.

"Can't tell you. If I tell you, I'd have—"

"To kill me. Yeah, yeah. Whatever." She rolled her eyes.

Hunter chuckled. "Can't give you all my secrets."

"You haven't given me any secrets. You're an enigma."

"Maybe there's nothing to tell."

"That I seriously doubt."

Hunter was about to respond when the front door open.

"Anybody home?" A male voice called from the living room.

Sable's eyes went wide, and she jumped up from the table. Hunter followed more slowly but arrived in time to see her rush into Hossam's arms and receive a big hug from his Arab friend. He lifted her off her feet.

Once again, the cut of jealousy twisted its sharp, jagged edge into his chest. Hunter despised his possessive feelings toward Sable. Helping her didn't give him a hold on this woman, so why did he want to club his friend over the head for a simple hug?

Hossam placed her back on her feet and cupped her face in his hands. He said something to her in French, and she replied, her voice soft and damn near coquettish. Excluded from the conversation, Hunter became annoyed and shoved his hands in his pockets.

The moments he and Sable had shared paled in comparison to the obvious affection between her and Hossam. Clearly, there was something going on between them.

Hossam approached Hunter with a smile and his hand extended. He was the same height as Hunter but with a wiry build and olive skin.

Both men shook hands, and Hossam clapped him on the shoulder.

"Good to see you, my friend," Hossam said.

"Likewise. I expected you tomorrow at the earliest."

"I finished up my business ahead of time and took an early flight back." His gaze slid to Sable. "I hear you've gotten yourself into a little trouble."

She grimaced and was the only woman Hunter had ever seen who looked adorable grimacing.

"A little is an understatement. Before we update you, are you hungry? Hunter made dinner, and there's plenty."

"Good, because I came straight here from the airport, and I'm hungry."

The three of them went into the kitchen, and as both men sat down, Sable spooned food onto a white plate for Hossam.

Hunter watched her fix his friend a plate and felt a twinge of... hell, he didn't like it. Preparing a man's plate wasn't a big deal, certainly not something he'd ever necessarily wanted, but watching her perform that small act of kindness for Hossam made him feel some kind of way.

"Any developments since we talked?" Hossam asked, his dark eyes landing on Hunter.

"We have so much to tell you," Sable said.

She set the plate of food and an opened bottle of Orangina in front of Hossam and then joined the men at the table. They updated Hossam on her dead friend and the fight for their lives in the basement of the cafe.

Stunned, Hossam didn't speak as he digested the retelling of the events. "A lot has happened since we talked," he said.

Hunter nodded. "I checked out the Bible to see if there was a note or something else hidden in the spine, but nothing. After dinner, Sable and I plan to go through each page to see if there's a code hidden in the passages."

"The Bible is written in Latin, correct?"

Hunter nodded.

"So either the code is hidden among the Latin—Latin itself —or it could be in another language, such as French or English."

Face pensive, Sable said, "We're hoping it's written in another language because neither of us knows Latin. Of course, we could reach out to someone who does speak the language, but without knowing for sure there's a hidden message, it seems like a waste of time."

"If they're smart, they would use Latin to hide the message. I would." Hossam cut into the tender meat and ate a piece.

"Then we need to find someone who can read it. Do you know anyone?" Sable asked.

"I can find someone through my contacts," Hossam said with utmost confidence.

"I have the license plate number of the BMW the men who attacked us were driving," Hunter said.

"I should be able to look into the ownership of the vehicle, through non-official channels, though. Since this isn't an official investigation, I'll have to call in some favors, but I'll do my best to help."

"Sable mentioned Moreau has come under investigation in the past, but he's never been convicted." Hunter sipped his wine.

Hossam nodded as he chewed. "He's probably paid people off. Law enforcement hasn't been able to link him directly to any wrongdoing. They suspect he's somehow involved in drug trafficking because of his relationship with a Corsican crime family, the Criminis, but the man is untouchable at this rate. A few years ago, his business was thoroughly investigated, and they found no evidence of illegal activity. They raided his warehouse once because of complaints of suspicious activity at night but found nothing incriminating."

"Where there's smoke, there's fire," Hunter said.

"I agree with you, but without evidence, nothing can be done. His paperwork is always in order, and his warehouse only contains legitimate goods. At this point, his lawyers can block future investigations. He has been investigated so many times and had the charges dismissed, the government is tiptoeing around him so as not to be seen as harassing a member of the business community."

"As you pointed out, practically untouchable," Hunter said.

Hossam swallowed a mouthful of soda and nodded. "Whatever crime or crimes he has committed, they cannot be found. They are invisible to the average investigator."

Sable, who sat quietly while they talked, suddenly perked up. "Oh my goodness, the answer has been right there under our noses the whole time. I can't believe I didn't figure it out before."

"What?" Hunter said.

She smiled slowly. "He used invisible ink."

15

They filed out the kitchen, with Hossam and Hunter trailing behind Sable. She picked up the leather bound Bible and faced them.

"I can't believe I didn't think of this before. When I broke into Moreau's house, his office was filled with George Washington memorabilia. He's kind of obsessed with the United States and its history and is a huge Washington fan. Which means he probably knows that during the Revolutionary War, Washington encouraged his agents to write invisible messages in the blank spaces of books."

"And you think that's the situation here?" Hossam asked with skepticism.

"It's a possibility." She looked from one to the other.

Hunter chimed in. "It would explain why they were so hell-bent on getting the Bible back."

Hossam stared at the Bible. "Okay, let's say you're correct. How do we figure out where in those hundreds of pages they placed the message?"

"I don't think they hid the message on the pages with text. The first five pages of the Bible are blank. There's nothing there, at least to the naked eye," Sable said. The more she thought about it, the more the idea made sense.

"Do you know how to uncover the message, assuming there is one?" Hunter asked.

"Heat." Sable said the word with a satisfied smile. "Do you have an iron?"

"There's one in the bedroom closet," Hossam interjected.

"Join me in the bedroom, gentlemen."

"Sounds kind of kinky," Hossam joked.

Sable tossed a flirtatious look over her left shoulder, and Hunter blew flames from his nostrils, grinding his teeth.

In the bedroom, Sable turned on the iron and carefully tore a page from the Bible. She spread the blank sheet on the bed and waited for the iron to get hot.

"How do you know this stuff?" Hunter asked, impressed.

"I told you, I'm a history buff. Ask me anything about American history, and I can answer your question."

Her excitement and cockiness were exciting to watch. This was her element, and the insecurity and fear from earlier were gone.

Sable gently smoothed the hot iron over the page. After a couple of swipes, two columns of numbers appeared on the paper.

"Hot damn," Hunter said. She was right.

Sable continued to work carefully.

When she finished, the entire page contained neat handwriting. The numbers on the left were all different, but the numbers in the right-hand column alternated between two different numbers.

The three of them stared at the information.

Sable broke the silence. "What do you think this means?"

Hunter pointed at the second column. "These are nine digits," he said.

"So? All the numbers on the left are..." Sable counted. "Twelve digits."

"Right, but they're all different, while there are only two different nine-digit numbers. The first thing that comes to mind is routing numbers."

Hossam nodded his head in agreement. "I was thinking the same thing." He pointed to the digits on the left. "I'm almost certain those are account numbers. Let's see which banks the routing numbers represent." He lifted out his phone.

Hunter waited anxiously for him to reveal the answer.

Hossam looked at both of them. "Banque Quotidienne."

"Both of them?" Hunter asked.

"Yes. It's the largest private bank in the country. These numbers represent the Paris and Panama branches."

"Let's finish and see if any other banks are included. Maybe that will help us figure out what's going on," Hunter said.

They spent the next twenty minutes watching Sable carefully work on the other blank pages. All the routing numbers pointed to Banque Quotidienne. Two pages in all, with the other three pages blank, perhaps waiting their turn to be filled.

"Again, what does this mean?" Sable asked.

"It could mean anything. Bank accounts where bribes have been sent, maybe?" Hunter said.

"If so, one of these accounts might belong to Richelieu. Bertrand accused him of being greedy and said there were many more where he came from. Richelieu was killed because he wanted more money. He thought he was indispensable, but Moreau might have dozens of people working for him," Sable said.

Hossam's expression was grim. He paced away from them, running his fingers through his black, curly hair.

"But it doesn't make sense they'd all have accounts at the same bank. Why not accept the bribes at their own bank?" Sable asked.

She had a point, which made Hunter pause. Then he gave a short laugh. "Because they could set off red flags at their own bank. People typically bank in Panama for two main reasons—the money is drug-related, or they're trying to avoid taxes. In this case, it could be simple tax evasion by multiple account holders. What if they're all using the same banker? Someone who's being paid to keep quiet."

Hossam swung to face him. "What you said makes sense. My friend in financial crimes could find out more about those accounts." He looked at his watch. "Can't do anything tonight, but tomorrow I'll start calling in those favors, and we should get some answers."

Sable stifled a yawn.

"Tired?" Hunter asked.

"A little. It's early though."

"You've had a long day. Trauma can take a lot out of you."

"What about you? You had the same day I did."

"I've learned to adapt."

"Sable, I could take you to my place, and we could let Hunter have this apartment," Hossam offered. "With only one bedroom, it must be difficult, and I have more room."

"Oh. I..." Her voice trailed off as she looked at Hunter.

He spoke up. "With her being wanted for murder, it's probably better if she stays here."

Hossam's gaze shifted between them, one eyebrow rising briefly. "Oh. Okay. Makes sense," he said, knowing good and well the explanation didn't make sense.

"Let's get out of here so she can go to bed."

Hunter gathered the Bible and torn out pages from the mattress.

"Thank you for the offer. *Bonne nuit.*" Sable gave Hossam a hug. She glanced at Hunter. "Good night."

"Good night." His eyes lingered on her for a moment before he followed Hossam out the door.

HUNTER CLIMBED through the window and onto the balcony. Hossam handed out a couple of chairs for them to sit on and then joined Hunter.

Hossam held another bottle of Orangina in hand, while Hunter placed a glass of wine on the ground and held an apple in his hand. Each time he cut a slice, he slipped a piece of fruit into his mouth.

"Your English has gotten a lot better," he remarked to his friend.

"I've been practicing, though I still think certain words are ridiculous. For instance, d-e-a-f spells deaf, but m-e-a-l spells meal. Why isn't it pronounced mel? Or deaf pronounced deef? You see the problem?"

Hunter chuckled. "I do. Then we have words such as enough and dough."

"Exactly!" Hossam used his bottle to point. "It's confusing, but practice makes perfect. I have greatly improved, as you've said."

"I'm jealous. I only speak English."

"Spend a few months in France, and you'll get better at speaking your mother's language."

Hunter winced at the comment. "Yeah," he said slowly.

"Have you found out anything else?" Curious eyes turned on him.

"Not much more than I knew when I arrived. She was an only child, and with her parents dead, there's no one."

For years he'd never known his background, but after spending time with Cruz Cordoba, the owner of The Cordoba Agency, and his family, Hunter became envious. Cruz had carved out a normal life for himself. Then another member of their team, Raheem, reconnected with a past love.

Hunter had always considered the people he occasionally

worked with on missions as close as he could get to family, but these people knew who they were and could share their history with loved ones. He didn't know his family and wondered about his background. Something he hadn't cared much about before. He'd sort of liked the anonymity and mystery, but no more. He wanted to know his roots and origin in preparation of sharing his past with someone.

Cruz helped him track down his parents. His father was Black and Native, his mother a French novelist who'd visited the States as a teen and become pregnant, leaving him with his father before returning to France. He didn't have much more information about her and had hoped to learn more during this trip.

"I'm sorry. What will you do now?" Hossam asked.

"There's one more piece of information I need to collect. I hope to have it before I leave for the States."

"I wish you luck."

"Thanks."

Hossam shifted in the chair and cleared his throat. "How is my friend?"

"Tell me you're not asking about Alissa." When Hossam smiled, Hunter shook his head. "I thought there was something going on between you and Sable. Did I read the situation wrong?" His muscles tensed.

"Yes, you did. She and I are nothing more than friends, believe me."

Relief shuddered through Hunter, but he remained calm, slicing into the apple and lifting the fruit to his lips. "How did the two of you meet?"

"Would you believe, I was looking for a piece for the apartment? I was at a flea market, trying to decide on an antique vanity set for my mother. Sable was at the same flea market, and I asked her opinion, to get a woman's point of view. She was so knowledgeable, I was impressed. To thank her for her help, I invited her to lunch, and we've been friends ever since."

"You didn't have a problem when you found out the type of work she does?"

Hossam snorted. "Who am I to judge?"

Hunter understood his reaction. Though Sable was a thief, he also found it hard to judge. For one, he hadn't exactly lived a pure life himself, and she used her skills to help people.

"So, did your mother like the vanity?"

"She loved it. She took it to Morocco when they retired." He side-eyed Hunter. "Are you going to tell me about Alissa?"

"You know better."

"I shouldn't ask about her?"

Alissa had been on the same mission in Morocco with Hunter and Hossam. Something happened between the two of them, but neither had divulged details about their relationship —*if* there had been a relationship. They neither confirmed nor denied when Hunter tried to find out. Their alleged affair was none of his business, but Alissa was like a sister to him. Although she could take care of herself, he didn't want anyone messing with her.

"She's doing okay," Hunter answered, purposely keeping his answer vague, though he knew what Hossam was really asking. He wanted to know if she was seeing anyone.

"Good."

"You seeing anyone?" Hunter asked.

"You know how it is. In our line of work, it's difficult to keep a relationship. Finding a partner who understands the work and why I travel so much, without telling them why, is impossible."

"Not to mention sometimes they can't reach you for days or weeks at a time."

"Months, if we're deep under cover," Hossam murmured.

"Ever thought of doing something else?" Hunter asked.

"Like you? Security?" He blew a raspberry. "Not for me, my friend."

"I used to think the same thing, but at some point, you'll have to slow down. We all do. Working a regular job, you at least have a chance at a real relationship. If you ever want to talk options, let me know."

Hossam's expression turned thoughtful as he gazed at the building across the street. "I will," he said.

They fell silent again, allowing the sounds of the city—car horns and bus motors—to fill the void between them.

After a while, Hossam came to his feet. "Tomorrow, I'll see what I can find out about the Moreau case."

"You're leaving already?"

"Afraid so. It has been a long day. Good night." Hossam opened the window and paused. "If Sable is in the bedroom, where are you going to sleep?"

"On the sofa." Hunter sipped his wine.

"You're sure?"

Hunter gave a short laugh. "Absolutely."

"Maybe if you ask nicely, she'll share the bed with you."

"I'll have to give that a try."

Hossam chuckled. "*Bonne nuit, mon ami.*"

"*Bonne nuit,*" Hunter returned.

16

The morning light sliced through the window and forced Sable to squint against its glare. She had slept late, dragged from a dream about Hunter into consciousness. In the vivid fantasy, he came into the room and joined her in the bed instead of sleeping on the sofa. Under the covers, he'd pried her thighs apart and guided his hard erection between her hips.

She rolled over and moaned, squeezing her knees together to stifle the pulsing, sticky spot between her legs, which only made the pulsing worse. Her nipples ached something awful. She rubbed the rigid peaks and then stopped. Nope, she was not doing that to herself—not getting herself off to thoughts of Hunter.

She'd half expected him to come into the bedroom after the look they exchanged when they convinced Hossam she didn't need to stay at his place. She should have taken her friend up on the offer, but then she wouldn't be near Hunter, an infinitesimally worse idea.

"Why, though?" she muttered. Why was being apart from him a worse idea?

She sighed. She barely knew Hunter and knew better than to let lust and a palpitating heart control her actions. She wanted love—the kind where your heart aches when you're apart from your other half. What would it be like to love so deeply and *be* loved deeply in return? To feel hollow when separated from the person you cared so much about. The beautiful agony of it all. She wanted that. Longed for it.

Sable dragged from the bed. After brushing her teeth and washing her face, she changed into jeans and a shirt and pulled her hair into a loose knot at the nape. She found Hunter in the living room, pacing the herringbone wood floor with a phone attached to his ear. He looked... delicious. He'd shaved, but his impressive jaw line remained shadowed, and his Olympian physique couldn't hide beneath a gray Henley and fitted jeans, filled out by his thick thighs and great butt.

Their eyes locked, and a shock jolted her heart as if she'd stepped on a downed power line.

"Sable is awake. I'll give her an update." He paused. "Yeah, of course. Talk to you later."

"Was that Hossam?" she asked, hooking a thumb in her belt loop.

He nodded. "His friend in financial crimes said the accounts all belong to Moreau. They're business accounts for his antique shops. Millions deposited every month, for years."

"So he's not bribing anyone?"

"Not through those accounts. Seems legit."

"Why does he need so many?"

"Don't know. The guy in financial crimes also found two other bank accounts in the name of Moreau's businesses, but they weren't on the list in the Bible. Millions passing through them too, but much less."

"So there's something special about the ones written in the Bible."

"Apparently."

Hunter folded his arms across his impressive chest. "We were right about one thing—one person at the bank is handling all the accounts. Guy by the name of Maximo Costas. He's a wealth manager and only deals with the bank's most affluent clients. Bad news on the license plate. The BMW was stolen and the plates belonged to a different car."

"It's obvious Moreau knows how to cover his tracks, so I'm not surprised his people know how to cover theirs." Sable gently cleared her throat. "I wanted to thank you for allowing me to stay here instead of shipping me off to Hossam's apartment, even though it means you have to continue to sleep on the sofa."

His mouth lifted at the corners into a roguish smile. "Maybe I like having you around, and sleeping on the sofa is a small price to pay for that luxury."

Butterfly wings fluttered in her stomach, and Sable experienced a feeling—a feeling of wanting his hands all over her. If he ever made a move, she was ninety-nine percent certain she couldn't resist him, and she needed to resist him. She did not want to be one of many conquests during his trip.

Before she could respond, Hunter added, "I asked Hossam about the location of Moreau's warehouse—the one where people complained about suspicious activity. I'm going to pay it a visit and take a look around inside."

"Can I come?"

Hunter picked up his bedding and moved pass her. "You need to stay here."

Sable followed him. "They killed my friend and blamed his death, as well as Senator Richelieu's death, on me. If there's dirt on Moreau in the warehouse, I want to help find it. Whether you approve or not, I'm coming."

Hunter placed the items on the bed and turned to face her. "I could tape you to a chair and leave you here."

"You could, but you won't." She challenged him with her eyes.

He pursed his lips. "No, I won't."

Sable breathed easier. She hadn't been one hundred percent sure he wouldn't do that.

He silently appraised her. "If you come, you do everything I say. No questions, no pushing back."

"Deal."

He came closer, and she held her breath as she gazed up at him.

"We go tonight."

He left the room, and she released a tremulous breath. Yeah, she should have gone to stay at Hossam's.

They spent the day conducting research.

Seated at the desk in the living room, Hunter pulled up satellite photos of the warehouse, located miles outside the city in an industrial park with twelve similar buildings.

"We could go through the front," he said, using the mouse to find different angles of the building, a huge two-story made of white brick. The flat roof was rimmed by a steel railing. The front of the building contained a one-story section consisting of the front entrance and some offices exposed by glass on three sides.

"Or we could go in through the roof." Sable pointed. "See, right there. A skylight."

Hunter zoomed in.

"We can use my crowbar to pry it open, and I have rope and a grappling hook with a collapsible claw to get us on top of the building."

Hunter twisted his head to look at her.

"What?"

"You're something else." He smiled and shook his head. "All right, we'll do it your way."

Next, they pulled up news articles and videos about Jean-

Jacques Moreau and his business activities. Hunter continued to use the computer, while Sable sat on the sofa and used her phone.

Moreau's social calendar remained full from dinner parties and other events occurring fairly frequently at his estate in the countryside. He also supported a long list of social causes and donated funds to various foundations, as well as—ironically, considering the allegations against him—a popular anti-drug campaign.

From the information they found, his wealth grew exponentially each year, starting approximately five years ago after the fraud uncovered at his company put him into a financial slump. Since then, he'd been photographed with celebrities and politicians, and his business had exploded in growth.

His wife was a gorgeous blond from California and twenty years younger than Jean-Jacques at thirty-four. She left Hollywood behind to marry him and move to France eight years ago.

Hunter dug up photos of Moreau, as well as information on the rumors of his illegal activities and the investigation of his company. What he found looked like an innocent man being harassed by the police. His publicists did a great job with the spin.

By late afternoon, Sable excused herself to take a break. She went into the bedroom and sat cross-legged on the mattress. She needed to talk to Avril, and at this hour in the States, her classes were finished for the day. She propped the phone on a pillow and dialed her daughter on FaceTime.

"Hi, honey." Sable waved and Avril waved back. She read lips but Sable preferred to sign whenever they talked.

Sable's nutmeg-brown skin was darker than her daughter's golden complexion, but they both had hazel eyes. Sable had been nervous when she dropped her off at the university in the fall—the first time they had been separated from each other for a significant period. She'd worried about Avril, though the entire university accommodated the hearing impaired.

She quickly learned *she* was the one with the problem and had nothing to worry about. Avril thrived in the new environment, enjoyed meeting other deaf kids and adults, and learned a lot in her classes.

"How is school? You ready for the semester to end?"

Avril grinned, nodding. "School has been excellent, of course. I passed my biology exam with a B plus," she signed. "I'm going into the end of the semester with all A's and B's, so I would say my first year as a college student is a win, especially after I tell you my big news." She looked about to burst with excitement.

"Tell me!"

Avril laughed. With a flurry of hand movements, she explained, "I'm going to Washington State to work for Microsoft! They're hiring hearing-impaired students to work on a top secret project. Another student dropped out, and Microsoft chose me to take his place in the program. Can you believe it?"

"That's wonderful! I'm so proud of you!"

Avril beamed her joy. "Thanks, I'm excited. If I do a good job, I could return every summer and possibly have an entry-level position when I finish school."

"They'll love you, and of course you'll do well. You work hard and you're smart."

Avril blushed. "Thanks, Mom."

Sable's heart ached at the thought of her all the way in Washington for an entire summer. No more lazy afternoons at the lake or girls' nights watching movies and eating popcorn until the early morning. Avril was growing up and forging her own path. Sadness tempered her joy at her daughter's achievements.

"What time is your flight tomorrow?" Avril asked.

"That's why I called. I have a little bit of bad news. Nothing tragic. I need to stay a little longer in France. I haven't found the piece I'm looking for, so I won't be back tomorrow as planned." She'd lied and told Avril the antique shop sent her to France to find a specific desk for a wealthy client.

Avril pouted.

"Something came up," Sable added quickly. What an understatement. "But I'll be back in time to pick you up from school and help you get ready for your summer job."

Avril frowned, her hands moving quickly as she tried to put Sable's mind at ease. "Don't worry about me. I'm busy with my friends and schoolwork. Enjoy your extra days. You're in France! Pretty soon you'll be making those trips for yourself when you open your own store."

"Yeah." Sable's spirits deflated. Opening her store wouldn't happen anytime soon because her million dollar payout no longer existed.

"Did I say something wrong?" Avril frowned into the camera.

Sable immediately perked up. She didn't want to worry her. "No, you didn't. And you're right, pretty soon I won't have to make these trips. Take care, and call me if you need anything."

"Of course. I love you." Avril held up the ILY handshape.

"Love you." Sable repeated the sign.

She blew her daughter a kiss, and their conversation ended.

17

Hunter handed Sable a black beanie. "We need to blend in as much as possible. The last thing we want is for anyone to recognize you as Veronica Shaw, the woman wanted for two murders and implicated in three others."

She couldn't believe she was wanted for murder. Except for a punch she'd thrown as a teenager when another teen made snide comments about her being a teenage mother—not her finest moment—she'd never committed an act of violence in her life.

She pulled the hat low on her head, tucking her hair under the edges.

Hunter's makeup kit lay open on the bed, and he removed the mustache and applied it to his upper lip. "Put on these sunglasses."

Sable took them and stared. "It's nighttime."

"You're wanted for murder. Sunglasses are the least of your problems."

Good point.

She settled them on her face and checked her appearance

in the mirror above the dresser. She wore dark colors like Hunter. No jewelry, no makeup.

"We want to make sure to keep a low profile. On the way to the warehouse—"

"I know how to keep a low profile. I'm a thief, remember?" Sable turned away from her reflection to face him.

He narrowed his eyes. "What did I say about no pushback?"

She fell silent and ignored the little thrill his commanding voice sent through her.

Hunter continued talking, offering advice as he put away his supplies and stuffed their tools in an Army-green canvas backpack he'd purchased earlier.

They took the subway to a station several stops away. When they exited at their destination, they strolled down a back street, looking for a car to steal. Hunter settled on an inconspicuous charcoal gray Renault. Sable got the door open, and he hot-wired the vehicle. Within minutes, they were driving out of the city toward the industrial park.

Sable removed the sunglasses and watched Paris go by as they left the city limits.

After a while, Hunter remarked, "You're awfully quiet. Sorry you came?"

"No, but I am wondering how this is going to end."

"With Moreau in jail, if I have anything to do with it," he said.

"I want him locked up more than anything." The rear lights of the vehicle in front of them kept her attention on the long highway. "I talked to my daughter today, and I'm worried."

He glanced at her. "Why?"

"Everything I do is for her because I want her to have a better life. I want her to be safe. I don't want my actions to affect her." She focused on his profile. "You know what I'm saying?"

"I understand what you're saying." He took her hand and gently squeezed. "We're going to get this guy before he ever has a chance to figure out who and where your daughter is. I promise." His eyes met hers for a split second before they returned to the road ahead.

Sable nodded, satisfied. The kindness in his voice comforted her, and his warm touch soothed her concerns. When he released her to return his hand to the wheel, she missed his touch and wished he'd continued to hold her. Hunter was a tough guy, but there was also a gentleness about him—a gentleness that called into question her adamant stance against getting involved with a man like him.

They pulled into the industrial park and drove slowly through the lot in search of building ten, Moreau's warehouse.

"There," Sable said, pointing.

Hunter nodded. Cars were parked outside, but no trucks pulled up to any of the three bays. As they drove by, two men smoked cigarettes outside the main door.

"They have security," Sable said. "I guess it makes sense since Moreau probably stores millions of dollars' worth of antiques in that warehouse."

The men watched the Renault go by, and Sable stopped looking, following Hunter's lead of keeping his eyes straight ahead, as if he didn't see the men.

"All these buildings have millions of dollars' worth of products in them, but none of the others have exterior guards, and those men are armed. I could tell by the bulge in their jackets."

They left the parking lot, and Hunter stashed the car half a mile away behind bushes.

"What are you going to do about the guys out front?" Sable asked.

Hunter climbed out of the car and slung the backpack over his shoulder. "Nothing. We're going in through the roof, so we don't have to worry about them unless we cause a disturbance and they have to investigate. I don't plan on causing a disturbance."

On a brisk walk, Hunter led the way and Sable followed, surveying the area from her position behind him. They arrived on the property in ten minutes and at the warehouse in another five. They approached it from the rear. No windows at the back. Hunter swung the rope with the grappling hook around and around to gain momentum, then flung it onto the top of the building. The claw clanged when it connected with the steel railing at the top.

They both didn't move for a few seconds to ensure they hadn't drawn attention. In the distance, a man's yelling voice drifted toward them on the wind, but the night remained still with the only other sounds that of cars passing on the highway nearby.

Hunter tugged the rope to test its sturdiness.

"It's good. You first," he said.

Sable fastened her fingers around the rope and hoisted herself up. She used the "brake and squat" technique of Navy Seals, letting the rope ride on the outside of her leg and pinching it between her feet—a faster and less tiring method of climbing that gave better control.

Hand over fist, she lifted higher until she reached the top of the building and hopped over the railing. Hunter followed next, using the same rope-climbing method, his height giving him an advantage. He reached the top in much less time than she did.

He pulled up the rope and wound it around his hand, then they jogged over to the skylight. He removed the crowbar from the sack, and with two hard thrusts opened the window without breaking it. They both blew out relieved breaths.

He flashed a pen light in the dark room below, which appeared to be an office. They listened for an alarm, and when none sounded, Hunter shimmied down the rope and dropped lightly to his feet. Sable followed behind him.

With Hunter leading the way, they crept to the door and

unlocked it from the inside. Hunter peered into the hallway of the eerily silent building.

They walked out, quiet on their feet and sticking close to the wall. About to round a corner, Hunter stopped suddenly, and Sable froze. He placed a finger to his lips and then gestured ahead with two fingers. She peeked around him and saw a security booth with a guard watching the monitors.

Hunter placed the sack on the floor. Staying low so the guard wouldn't see him through the glass, he duck-walked to the door.

He entered so suddenly, the poor man didn't have time to react. He turned in the chair, and Hunter's jab hit him dead between the eyes. His head snapped back and his arms fell to his sides. Unconscious.

Hunter handcuffed both hands around the leg of the table and set his radio on the opposite end of the room, out of reach. He then taped his mouth closed and switched off the monitors.

He signaled to Sable, and she met him at the door with the sack.

Their search of the upstairs proved fruitless. Mostly storage rooms and offices with file cabinets filled with invoices and freight documentation.

"There's nothing here," Sable whispered, disappointed. She didn't know what she'd expected, but they hadn't stumbled across anything incriminating yet.

"Let's keep looking. His business is not on the up and up. We both know that. If the problem isn't here, then at least we've eliminated this location and can search elsewhere."

Positive thinking. She needed to remember that.

They crept down the stairs, careful to listen for footsteps and voices that indicated others nearby. She heard faint laughter from the two men outside.

At the bottom of the stairs, Hunter peered around the

corner and signaled for her to follow. She came up close behind him.

"On the count of three, we rush across the open space," he said.

Sable prepared herself, muscles coiled for action. Hunter held up one finger and started the countdown.

One... two.... three. They sprinted across the open foyer. On the other side, they skidded to a stop and waited. Sable modulated her ragged breathing. No sound came from the direction of the men, so they hadn't been discovered.

They searched the rooms, breaking into the locked ones. Finally, they found a large storage space filled with unboxed items and sealed boxes.

Hunter tore open a box with his switchblade and examined the contents. He pulled out an old clock and some other objects.

Sable also opened a box and found copper and bronze statues. Walking around the huge space, she scanned shelves filled with framed art and vintage posters. She found Japanese porcelain and musical instruments—some in good condition, others in poor condition.

"Nothing here looks out of the ordinary. This is normal inventory," Sable said. She restlessly lifted a silver teapot and set it back down on the tray.

Hunter took a closer look at the labels on the boxes. "These are going out to shops around the city."

"His shops. If he's doing something illegal, I don't see it." She was hard pressed to keep the frustration out of her voice.

"I've seen enough. Let's get out of here," Hunter said.

As they approached the door, voices came from the hallway, and a shadow passed across the window in the door. Sable froze and held her breath. Were they coming in here?

The voices of two men, laughing and talking, headed toward the front of the building.

"Shift change, probably," Hunter said in a low voice.

Sure enough, more men came down the hall from the direction of the front door, their voices carrying as they walked.

Hunter cracked the door and peered out. "They went through the door at the end of the hall."

"Should we check it out?" Sable asked.

"Since we're here, we might as well. Stay close," he warned.

18

They moved quietly toward the door, and Hunter glanced over his shoulder in case other people started down the stark hallway. He turned the door-knob, but it was locked.

Sable dropped in front of it and did her thing while he was the lookout. When she opened the door, they slipped into another hallway, as stark and plain as the other, but darker and narrower.

Winding metal stairs led to a lower level, and they took their time creeping down to make as little noise as possible. At the bottom, voices came toward them, and Hunter dragged Sable into a shadowy corner and held her close, hiding her body with his. Her soft curves pressed into his chest and thighs and made his body stir. He swallowed the tightness in his throat, begging his wayward dick to behave because this was neither the time nor place to act up.

The men passed by and climbed the metal stairs, and Hunter relaxed his hold. For an awkward moment they looked at each other, Sable's eyes gazing up into his, her palms flattened on his chest. He abruptly released her and spun around to check the corridor.

Without another word, they slipped out of the corner and continued walking until they encountered steel double doors with a camera above them. He didn't worry because he'd turned the cameras off. Hunter eased one of the doors open.

Sable waited behind him, but when he slipped in, she silently followed. Inside, they dashed into the shadows and hid behind stacked boxes. Sable let out a soft gasp, and Hunter's mouth fell open at the sight before them.

In the center of the space, bright lights shone down on a flurry of activity. They were counting money. Loads of it getting pulled from boxes. Men and women stood in front of money-counting machines on long tables, sticking pile after pile of bills into the machines to be counted and sorted. A freight elevator had brought the boxes down from the delivery bay. Two men with Kalashnikov rifles patrolled the perimeter of the group.

"Why is all this money here?" Sable whispered.

"This is absolutely not normal. If I had to guess, I'd say this is a money laundering operation." Hunter snapped photos, using the zoom function on the phone's camera to get close-ups of the activity.

"I never expected this," Sable said.

"Me either, but now everything is starting to make sense." Hunter dropped behind the boxes next to Sable. "The millions of dollars going into separate accounts, his relationship with a drug dealer who's supposedly a client and lover of antiques. He's got to be laundering money for the Crimini family. Let's get out of here before we get caught."

They slipped out. Hunter quietly closed the door and tucked the phone in the backpack.

"Hey!"

They both swung around. A burly man dressed in dark

clothes glared at them. A quick sweep of his appearance, and Hunter noted he wasn't armed.

He dropped the bag and charged him. They crashed into the wall, two huge masses of muscle grunting in a struggle for dominance. The man swung a fist toward Hunter's face, but he blocked the blow with his left hand and swiftly followed with a punch to the jaw, knocking him sideways. The man fired back with a fist aimed toward Hunter's head, but Hunter ducked and landed a jab to his stomach and then a hard uppercut that cracked the man's jaw and sent him crashing to the hard floor.

But the damage was done. One of the men inside must have heard the commotion and popped open the door, gun ready. Hunter nabbed the muzzle. Simultaneously, he grabbed the back of the man's head and yanked the gun and the man's head downward. His knee swung up and connected with the man's chin. He howled in pain. An elbow to the back of his head forced him to the ground. Rifle now in possession, Hunter dropped the butt on the back of the man's head and knocked him unconscious.

"Let's go!" he said in a fierce whisper.

Weapon in hand, Hunter ran in the direction they'd come from. They scrambled up the stairs and into the dark hallway, bolting toward the door they'd entered to get to the lower level.

As they neared the open foyer, he heard the screech of radio communication. He didn't need to understand what they were saying to know the men downstairs were warning the men up here about their escape.

"Stay behind me," Hunter said as he crept closer to the wide open foyer.

He needed to move fast, or they'd soon be sandwiched between the guards at the front and the men at the back.

He pulled Sable low to the floor with him. Her loud breathing distracted him, and he lifted a finger to his lips to indicate she should be quiet. He needed to hear.

Immediately, she clamped a hand over her mouth and quieted her breathing, staring at him with scared eyes. He couldn't comfort her at the moment, though. He needed to keep them alive.

Hunter stood to his full height and cocked his head, listening for movement. Then he heard it. Footsteps. Barely audible. More than one person. The first guards they spotted upon entering the industrial park had carried handguns. He expected these new ones did too, while the automatic rifle in his hands fired six hundred rounds a minute. He held the advantage but still needed to be careful.

He swung his hand around the wall and fired in a wide sweep. The sound of breaking glass filled his ears with the constant bang of the weapon's release. After several seconds, he peered around the wall. One man down with blood pooling beneath him, but the other fired at Hunter, and the round clipped the wall near his head.

Hunter dropped back and went low. Damn! That was close. On his knees, he darted from behind the wall and fired twice. One bullet hit the man in the center of his chest. Hunter fired again, and the second shot sliced through his throat. He collapsed, dead.

"Hunter!" Sable screamed. Two men came running toward them. Before they could fire, Hunter rolled onto his back, pulled the trigger on the rifle and sent them scurrying behind the door.

"Let's go!" He hopped to his feet, and they raced across the open foyer, feet crunching on broken glass. They sailed through the doorframe and into the parking lot.

Pop. Pop.

Probably the men from downstairs.

Hunter stopped and swung around. "Keep going!" he yelled at Sable. He sprayed the building with rounds, forcing their pursuers to dive for cover behind the walls.

The gun clicked. The magazine was empty. *Goddammit!* He tossed the weapon.

Adrenaline soaring through his veins, he sprinted after Sable up ahead. She glanced back and saw him following.

As a semi-truck rumbled by, Hunter got an idea.

"Sable, get on the truck!"

He pumped his legs faster, long strides eating up the short distance and passing by her. He hopped onto the underride guard and grabbed the steel handle on the back.

Sable raced after him, but the men from the warehouse burst from the destroyed entrance of the building. Oh no. His heart started an anxious gallop in his chest.

Hunter stretched a hand to her. "Come on!"

In the darkness, he saw her struggling, face made up in a grimace of monumental effort, arms and legs pumping fast.

"Come on, babe. You can do it," he said in a low voice, reaching as far as he could.

Gunshots cracked in the night air, and he ducked. One of the bullets pierced the door inches from his shoulder.

He crouched lower, stretching his fingers toward Sable. If she didn't reach him soon, he'd have to jump off because he couldn't leave her behind.

"You can do it," he yelled.

Finally, they touched, but at the same exact moment, a round grazed his upper arm. The site of impact burned, like a hot poker being applied to his skin. He flinched and let her go, and she cried out in frustration.

Hunter stretched for her again, and their fingers connected. Ignoring the burn in his arm, he gripped her hand and yanked her toward him.

"Come on," he groaned, gritting his teeth with the effort.

Stretched as far as he could possibly go, only his fingertips gripped the metal handle and kept him from falling off. Using enormous effort, he dragged Sable toward him again. With the additional momentum, she catapulted forward and hopped onto the underride guard with him.

Yes! Finally. Thank goodness.

He stepped behind her and bracketed her body with his to protect against the shots being fired. Panting hard, she rested her forehead against the truck door.

Impulsively, Hunter kissed the top of her head, relieved she was safe. A quick glance over his shoulder showed the men had fallen behind and stood in the lot gazing after them.

Hunter dropped his lips to her ear. "We're jumping, on *go*."

Sable nodded.

The truck slowed as it turned a corner.

"Go!"

They jumped off. With a quick roll to lessen the impact, they hopped to their feet without missing a beat and ran toward the bushes on the side of the road.

They tramped through the brush back to the car and stopped for a moment to catch their breaths. Hunter braced his hands on the trunk, and Sable dropped her butt to the bumper and buried her head in her hands, breathing hard.

After a minute, Sable lifted her head, and her eyes widened. "You're hit."

"Flesh wound," Hunter answered. Blood trickled down his arm inside the sleeve, and the wound throbbed.

She stood. Frowning, she touched his black shirt, soaked with blood where the bullet had torn through the fabric.

"Don't worry about my minor injury. We need to go."

"Hunter—"

"Let's *go*. No arguing."

She bit her lip and swung away from him, and they hopped in the vehicle.

Once they hit the highway, Hunter dialed Hossam's number. "Sable and I just left Moreau's warehouse, and we've figured out what he's up to. Money laundering. They're transporting cash. Truckloads of it. He must be using the trucks from his antique company to pick up the cash and carry it to the warehouse. The funds then go through Costas at the bank. We have pictures of the operation."

"You're kidding! Send them to me as soon as you can."

"I'm driving. I'll get Sable to do it."

"Hunter, thank you so much! My friends in financial crimes will be ecstatic. I'll work with them and law enforcement to push for a warrant to search the premises before they shut down the operation. That's clearly what happened before. I'll be in touch."

As Hunter drove, Sable sent the photos to Hossam. The whole time he drove, he kept his gaze on the rearview mirror, hoping they'd completely outrun the men back at the warehouse.

Only when they broke the city limits did Hunter relax. He parked the car in a low traffic part of Saint-Germain, careful to wipe down the steering wheel, trunk, and handles. They headed back to the apartment, trying to be unobtrusive as they walked behind buildings and out of the well-lit areas because of his blood-soaked sleeve. The black shirt hid that it was blood, but there was a large wet spot on his arm.

After twenty minutes, they arrived at the building. A male tenant brushed past on his way out as they entered. His gaze rested on Hunter's wet arm and the torn sleeve, and he frowned.

Hunter's heart jumped, but he behaved normal. "*Bonne nuit*," he said in a friendly voice.

"*Bonne nuit*," the man said, glancing at Sable in her beanie and sunglasses. He continued into the street.

Inside the apartment, Sable pulled off the hat and glasses and collapsed against the door. "What a night. That was close," she said.

"Yeah."

Hunter approached her and rested a hand against her soft cheek. Adrenaline still laced his blood, keeping him wired. The night's excitement made him want to kiss her to expunge the pent-up energy.

Instead, he asked, "You okay?"

She swallowed, looking up at him through her thick, curly lashes. Heat surged in his blood. If she kept looking at him with those sultry eyes, he wouldn't be responsible for his actions.

"I'm fine. You're the one who got shot."

"It hurts, but it's not bad." He examined the cut through the hole in his shirt. The bullet had scraped off the skin, leaving a red, inflamed gash.

"That looks bad, Hunter."

"It's fine. I'll clean up in the bathroom."

He headed in that direction and pushed open the door, first removing the fake mustache. Under the sink he found a first aid kit and placed it on the counter. He found a bottle of ibuprofen and dry-swallowed a couple of pills to diminish the throb in his arm.

Then he removed gauze and antiseptic from the kit to take care of the wound.

19

"Let me help you," Sable said from the doorway.

"I got it. I've been shot before. I have nine lives." Hunter flashed a grin.

Her hand grasped his undamaged arm. "Please."

He paused. "All right." He turned down the lid on the commode and sat down.

"Take off your shirt," Sable instructed as she doused a washcloth with warm water.

Hunter pulled the shirt over his head and revealed his firm chest. Blood stained his sandy-colored skin and the blond hairs on his forearm.

Sable started cleaning his arm and around the cut. "Why do you do this?"

"Do what?" So close to him in the small bathroom, his voice rumbled in her ears.

"You're good at what you do, but you risk your life to protect people all the time, right? How can you constantly jeopardize your own safety?"

"You're one to talk."

She looked up at him briefly before setting the bloody rag

on the counter and picking up a cotton swab. "Normally, being a thief isn't so dangerous."

He watched her work for a bit. "It's exciting. It's in my blood. I've been this way since I was sixteen. I got into trouble and an organization helped me get on the right path."

"Men like you..." Sable shook her head, tossing the bloody cotton in the trash. "Never mind."

"Men like me? Daredevils?" he prodded.

"Yes, daredevils. And players."

"What's wrong with us? Daredevils are fun. Players make the best lovers." Amusement filled his voice.

She wrapped his arm with gauze, keeping her eyes trained on the task and avoiding his eyes. "Players also break hearts."

"Only if you give them your heart," Hunter said in a low voice.

That was a warning if she ever heard one. Sable smoothed a hand over the bandage. "There." She briefly washed her hands while he continued to watch her.

When she finished, she stepped back, but Hunter caught her shirt and held her in place. She didn't want to look at him but couldn't resist lifting her gaze.

"You want to give me your heart, Sable?"

The thinning of the air made breathing difficult. "I'm not that foolish."

Hunter's light-colored eyes scoured her face. Then he stood, fisting her shirt in his hand and hauling her closer. Sable let out a soft gasp. The breath leaving her nostrils trembled and stuttered as much as her beating heart.

"Thank you for taking such good care of me."

She swallowed. "You're welcome."

He cocked his head, gaze dropping to her parted lips. "I've been wanting to kiss you for the longest. You gonna let me kiss you, Sable?" he asked huskily.

He didn't wait for an answer.

He dipped his head, and her lips fell open wider before his mouth touched hers. Their mouths crashed together, guttural moans leaping from their throats and filling the small bathroom.

Hunter took her hand and placed it over his erection. She whimpered and cupped his engorged manhood. Big. Hard. Deliciously thick. She wanted it. Needed it. Pounding her into the mattress.

The hunger for him tore her up inside, a river of need crashing against her insides and shoving her inhibitions out of the way.

He scooped her up with one fluid movement as their tongues touched, dancing around each other in a probing kiss. Trembling fingers traveled up the slope of his strong neck and onto his head. She took pleasure in touching him so freely, caressing his warm skin and soft, curly hair.

Hunter marched through the open door and into the bedroom and placed her on the bed. Hungry eyes looked down at her before he unsnapped the button on her dark jeans and pulled down the zipper. He hooked his fingers in the waistband and tugged them and her panties down at the same time.

One after the other, he kissed her calves and ankles. He murmured something she couldn't understand and kept on kissing all the way down to the soles of her feet. When he finished, he smoothed his hands up her thighs and forced her legs open. He kissed her sensitive skin and swiped his tongue along her slit.

Sable jerked at the fleeting touch. When he licked her again, her brain shut down. He groaned and allowed his tongue to dally on the tight nub between her thighs and gently scraped his teeth along her swollen labia in a torturous move that drove her mad.

Her belly trembled when his tongue swirled around her navel and his mouth traveled over the plane of her tight abs. At the same time, he pushed her shirt higher. Desperate for more of his touch, she wiggled out of the top and pulled it over her head as he unsnapped the front of her bra. Tossing the lingerie, his eyes focused on her chest. Her nipples tightened, and when his mouth fastened over her left breast, a shuddering moan left her throat.

She'd dreamed of this moment.

Desire ran rampant through her blood as his kisses scorched her skin, and every part of her cried out for more. His moist tongue swirled over her nipples and laved the entirety of her breasts, and she arched her back to go deeper into his mouth. He took his time on her breasts, sucking on the nipples and showering kisses on the sides and all over until she spread her legs and twisted beneath him with urgency.

He turned her over and gave the rest of her body the same treatment. Her back and bottom experienced the pressure of his teeth and the deep strokes of his fingertips. He was thorough and focused, making sure not a single inch of flesh remained untouched by his mouth and hands. It was almost more than she could stand, her nerve endings inflamed and her body trembling as she moved restlessly on the soft sheets.

Hunter practically pushed his face in her ass and tongued her clit from behind. Sopping wet, Sable gasped and moaned as he licked and sucked, her thigh muscles quivering under the onslaught. She clawed the sheets and angled her hips higher so he could get as much as he wanted.

When he lifted off her, she almost cried. She wanted more and had practically soaked the cover where her juices dribbled onto the fabric. Over her shoulder, she saw Hunter strip out of his clothes and toss them to the floor in utter disregard. He joined her on the bed and turned her over. His weight pressed down on her, his hardness hot and heavy against her stomach.

He kissed her earlobes and her neck and her breasts and her belly. He kissed the inside of her forearm and elbow. He twisted her body anyway he chose, uncaring of her half-hearted protests as he dragged her to the edge of self-control with rough hands.

Hunter stuffed two pillows under her bottom and elevated her hips, practically serving her up on a platter for his mouth.

With a devilish smile, he licked his lips. "You taste so damn good I can't stop eating you."

He kissed the plane of her stomach before diving between her legs again. She whimpered and thrashed beneath him, grabbing the back of his head to force him to stay in place.

But he refused, and by the time he worked his way back up to her mouth, she was a moaning mess, clawing at his shoulders and wrapping her legs around his waist—desperately needing the release he refused to grant her.

She begged him to let her come, but her pleading cries were met with shaky laughter.

"Wait a minute, babe," he said huskily.

He untangled himself from her limbs and retrieved several condoms from his wallet. Once he covered himself in protection, he planted his mouth over hers and guided his fullness to her entrance. Cupping her ass, he spread her thighs around his hips and shoved in with a smooth stroke.

"*Hunt—*" His half spoken name was a broken cry as she arched back against the blinding pleasure of having him fill her.

She shuddered. Stretched to the max and forced to endure as he took his time and made sure she became accustomed to his stroke.

"You good?" he asked hoarsely in her neck.

Her answer was a trembling moan.

He lifted his head and look into her eyes. "Is that a yes?"

"Yes. *Yes!*"

"Can I go deeper? Tell me I can go deeper, babe," he panted.

"Yes, please. Go dee—" she cried out as he did, plunging into her soaked depths.

His thrusting, gyrating hips sent her head spinning.

Making love to him was an experience. As he fucked her, his hands never stopped moving. They roved over her breasts, skimmed her sides, and gripped her ass cheeks. When he stretched her arms above her head and held them down with one hand, she thought she'd died and gone to heaven.

His free hand pushed one knee into her chest, and he sucked on her neck and her arched throat. All the while his hips undulated in a sensuous motion.

"Good girl. Take all this dick."

Held down, she was unable to move. Hips elevated on the pillows, body sloped backward in an elongated stretch. At the mercy of his brute strength. Overstimulated. Feeling him everywhere.

Sable *loved* it. Loved being pinned under him. Loved being bent to his will and subjected to his needs. Loved the way her hips were at the perfect angle to take his thrusts.

Hunter talked in her ear too.

One minute he was sweet. "So fucking beautiful. Look at you. So damn sexy."

The next minute he was nasty. "Goddamn, you're so wet. I know you love this. My dick is drowning in this wet pussy."

In the throes of passion, she watched in fascination as his narrowed eyes darkened from gunmetal gray to shadowy slate. Their fused bodies rocked together in unison. A perfect rhythm of thrusting hips. The clawing, aching, pulsing need inside her would finally be satisfied.

Hunter twisted his hips and hit her G-spot. Not once, but twice. Warmth spread through her in waves, and cries of ecstasy sliced the air.

Then Sable spasmed and abandoned herself to an all-consuming pleasure.

THEY LEFT the bed and took a shower together. When she returned to the bedroom, Hunter went to the kitchen and brought back snacks—fruit, cheese, crackers. They fed each other, and she fell out laughing when he grumbled about her messy eating habits causing crumbs to fall on the sheets.

Soon however, the food was gone, the laughter dried up, and only arousal remained. This time, Sable took the initiative and explored him at her leisure. Her lips brushed his, and they breathed the same air, soft pants and gentle kisses escalating into sensual need.

She ran her hands over his chest and encountered the steady beat of his heart. Her fingers coasted over his muscular arms and thighs, and her tongue licked his cucumber-mint scented skin. He was a sexy hunk of a man. Perfection. His body contoured with muscle and firm but soft skin. Not only smooth surfaces but rougher textures where dark blond hair covered his chest, arms, and thighs.

Their exploration of each other's body continued unabated. His fingers clutched her hair. His hands shaped the curves of her waist and palms smoothed over her bottom. In turn, she stroked his hard length and kissed his neck, hauled her fingers down his butt cheeks and kissed the old scar on his thigh where a bullet had entered his body.

Dragging her tongue along his Adonis belt, she listened to him inhale sharply. She took the mushroom-shaped tip of his erection into her mouth and sucked it like a popsicle on a hot summer day. His audible moans increased in volume the harder she sucked and pulled him deeper into her mouth.

She wanted to give pleasure as much as she received it. They'd only known each other days, but their lovemaking seemed long overdue, as if making up for lost time.

When Hunter slid between her thighs, his chest to her

back, hands cupping her breasts, she pressed her face into the pillow. He seemed to be everywhere—over her, under her, inside her. She gave body over to his powerful strokes. She purred her pleasure as her feminine muscles gripped him. Each whispered word made her wetter. Each thrust brought her closer to a climax. Until she could no longer resist and gave herself over to another exquisite orgasm that left her panting and trembling beneath him.

20

Gentle tapping on Jean-Jacques Moreau's bedroom door woke him from a light sleep.

"Who is it?" he called out.

"It's me, sir. You have a phone call." A male member of his nighttime staff spoke from the opposite side of the door. Jean-Jacques didn't want phone calls or text messages waking him up at inopportune times, so at night a trusted member of his staff answered calls and monitored texts in case of emergencies.

"Take a message!" he shot back, annoyed.

"It's Mr. Crimini, sir."

At the mention of the drug lord's name, he sat up in bed. He didn't often hear from the head man himself, so this must be important.

Jean-Jacques flipped on the bedside lamp, unconcerned about disturbing anyone else because his wife had started sleeping in a separate room a long time ago. He'd drawn the line when she allowed her dog to spend the night in bed with them. She showed more affection to the damn dog than she did him. To think they'd only been married eight years and already lived like strangers. Was it any wonder he sought attention elsewhere?

"Come in," he called.

The male staff member entered and handed him the phone. After he left, Jean-Jacques put the phone to his ear. "Hello?"

"What the hell is going on?" Elan growled.

He frowned. Granted, Elan Crimini was the one with the money, but he didn't appreciate being disrespected. He was, after all, an integral part of the man's operation.

"What are you upset about?" he asked.

"Don't tell me you're not aware."

Jean-Jacques fought hard not to scream obscenities into the phone. "No, I'm not aware," he said evenly.

"You had visitors at the warehouse tonight. They entered through the skylight and went snooping. They discovered the money. My men tried to detain them, but they killed two and injured several others. I was told the culprits were a man and a woman."

Jean-Jacques's heart jumped. "A Black woman?"

"Yes. Why?"

"I believe she's the one who broke into my home office and murdered Senator Richelieu."

Could the same woman—Vanessa Shaw—and her male companion be at it again? This time they broke into his warehouse. What prompted them to go there? What did they know?

Though Jean-Jacques leased the space, Crimini handled security because the money belonged to him, and he wanted to ensure the seamless transition of cash and make sure every dollar was accounted for.

His people used a variety of firearms but preferred the Kalashnikov rifle, like many of the Corsicans. How did men armed with such a powerful weapon manage not only to lose the man and woman but get killed in the process? This couple was not only tenacious, they were downright dangerous.

"We have to put a stop to this woman. She's clearly dangerous," Crimini said, echoing his concerns.

You have no idea, Jean-Jacques thought. He'd fed the
Corsican the same information he'd told the police. An
intruder broke into his home office during a dinner party.
Senator Richelieu went to his office to make a personal phone
call and encountered the thief, who then murdered the politi-
cian. With the senator being a small man, no one questioned
how such a small woman could get the upper hand and
strangle him.

Publicly, Jean-Jacques admitted to four thousand dollars in
stolen euros, but a select few knew about the Bible and the
incriminating information hidden in the front pages. If
Crimini knew the whole story, he'd put a bullet in Jean-
Jacques's head.

"Stopping her will be difficult. She's clearly not working
alone and can't be found," he said.

"Anyone can be found. What about your contacts at the
police department?" Crimini asked.

"What about yours?"

"This is your mess, Moreau. *You* clean it up."

Crimini never raised his voice, but there was no disguising
the fury and frustration dripping from each syllable. Up until
now, their business arrangement worked well, but this woman's
antics created cracks in their relationship.

"I'll see what I can do," he promised.

"Don't see what you can do. Fix it."

Crimini hung up, and Jean-Jacques stared at the phone. He
gripped it in a tight fist, tempted to toss the device across the
room.

Standing, he paced the carpeted floor of the opulent
bedroom decorated in a Victorian style. His wife's decision. All
of a sudden, the floral wallpaper irked him to no end. He hated
the huge four-post bed of dark wood he slept in alone, and he

hated the heavy linens. One day he'd redecorate the entire suffocating room.

He made a call and demanded his people collect the cash and move to another location for the time being, then instructed them to have a cleaner go in and clean up whatever mess there was. If Crimini's men were already there—which they probably were—his people knew to defer to them, but he reminded them, nonetheless.

Then he took a deep breath. "Think, think," he muttered. He didn't want to miss anything. Too much at stake.

He'd never been one to panic, but no way he was going back to a life of struggle. He carried a lot of shame growing up. Many nights he'd gone to bed hungry, and other kids had made fun of him because he wore shoes with holes in the soles and his older brothers' hand-me-downs. Today, he wore tailored suits from British and Italian designers, and he dined on Wagyu beef and caviar-topped desserts served in crystal goblets.

He was a king among men, respected in business and political circles. He would not allow a meddlesome little American woman to destroy everything he'd worked so hard for.

If he was being honest, he needed to expand beyond the Crimini family—a thought that came to him more often of late. Bad idea to put all his eggs in one basket, even if the basket gave him an abundance of money and prestige over the years.

He dialed the number for his assistant, Philippe. Though it was the middle of the night, he answered on the second ring.

"Did you know about the warehouse?" Jean-Jacques demanded by way of greeting.

"I did, and—"

"Why didn't I know about it?" He stopped pacing in the middle of the room.

"I was about to call you." Philippe spoke in an annoyingly calm voice.

"You're late. Crimini called already, and he's not pleased."

"I'm sure he's not," Philippe murmured.

"We have to work fast. I've already reached out to the team to clean up the mess at the warehouse, but I want *you* to go over there tonight and make sure everything is done to my satisfaction. I also want you to call our friends at the police department and tell them to do their fucking job. They need to find the Bible and that bitch. It shouldn't be this hard. Her picture was plastered all over the news."

Philippe cleared his throat. "Sir, the police don't have much to go on. The passport is a fake. They found her rental near the cafe, but that was also a dead end. No hits on any of the fingerprints in the vehicle."

Jean-Jacques let out an exaggerated sigh. "Bertrand shouldn't have killed the antique dealer. He should have kept him alive to pull more information from him."

Philippe didn't reply, his silence indicating he agreed. They'd often disagreed about Bertrand's tactics, with Philippe pointing out the big man tended to escalate violence while Jean-Jacques appreciated Bertrand did anything asked of him.

"I won't be able to sleep tonight. Keep me posted on everything that's happening. Next time we talk, I want good news."

"What do you consider good news, sir?"

"The money has been moved, the Bible has been found, and Vanessa Shaw and her boyfriend are dead. Clear enough for you?"

"Yes, sir. I'll get to work right away."

21

A fter a brief nap, Sable woke up in bed alone. Darkness still blanketed the city, but an atmospheric shift portended rain in the air. She brushed cracker crumbs off her breasts onto the floor and laughed to herself.

Stretching in the soft linens, memories of her and Hunter screwing flooded back. Sex the first time had been animalistic and out-of-control but so good. They'd needed to release the tension and displace the adrenaline from their run from the warehouse. The second time they touched each other with slower, more exploratory caresses.

So much for resisting him. She giggled and combed her fingers through her messy hair.

The door cracked open, and Hunter entered the room naked, dick slinging, munching on a peach. His body was a thing of beauty, cords of muscle in his arms and legs.

"You're awake," he said, rounding the bed to the side nearest the window.

"Mhmm." Sable's eyes followed his movement as he climbed into bed with her.

He offered the fruit, and she sat up and sank her teeth right next to where his mouth had touched. The oddly intimate bite made her lower body come alive, tingling with renewed desire. Sweet juice dribbled down her chin, but before she could wipe her face, Hunter dropped his head and licked it away with the tip of his tongue. Then he sucked her skin, as if to make sure he captured every drop, and moved his lips higher to suck her lower lip for several heart-stopping seconds.

"I think I got it all," he said huskily, a mischievous glint in his eyes.

She playfully shoved his chest. "The juice was on my *chin*," she said.

"And your lip. I could see it but you can't, and I like to be thorough."

He dropped another kiss to her mouth, angling his head to take his fill before withdrawing and leaving her breathless and on edge.

Hunter sat up against the headboard and took another bite of the fruit.

"You're always eating." Sable sat up, wedging the pillows behind her back.

"I have a high metabolism."

"And a lot of energy."

He arched an eyebrow. "Think you can keep up?"

"I'd like to try," Sable said, biting her bottom lip. "Hey, I want to ask you something, but I don't know if you'll be honest."

"Ask me anything. I have no reason to lie."

"Except about your occupation."

"I've never lied about that. I just couldn't answer your questions."

"Okay, let's skip conversations about your job. Why don't you want to share your personal life with me?"

Hunter finished eating the fruit and placed the pit on the nightstand on a napkin he'd brought in.

He slipped deeper under the covers and wrapped his arms around her waist, drawing her back against him.

"Mmm." Sable pushed back her hips so her bottom nested in the angle of his pelvis.

He kissed the side of her neck and slid a knee between her legs, simultaneously smoothing a hand down her thigh.

"You're going to make me hard again, and I don't think you're up for what I have in mind." His voice was low, and his breath warm on her ear.

Sable ran a hand down his hair-sprinkled forearm. "You're deflecting, Mr. Miller."

"Oh, I am, huh?" He sucked her shoulder blade.

She squirmed, and the room filled with the sound of her laughter. "*Quit.*"

They finally settled down with him pressed against her spine, as close as possible without joining their bodies. Outside, rain fell from the sky in a blitz of drops and lulled her into a relaxed state.

"Hunter, talk to me," Sable said in a soft voice. She felt a deep connection to him and wanted to know everything.

Threading his fingers through hers, he didn't answer right away. "It's hard to explain." Finally, he rolled onto his back with a heavy sigh and stared up at the ceiling.

Sable twisted to face him. "Try."

His chest deflated as he pushed air from his lungs. "There's a lot I don't know, and for the longest time, I didn't care to know. I figured I was alone in the world for a reason, and not knowing much about my past gave me an air of mystery."

"You didn't wonder?"

He frowned briefly. "I did from time to time, but you have to understand... it didn't matter because of the work I used to do. You know how earlier you mentioned you were worried about Moreau finding out about your daughter?"

"Yes."

"Not having a family made me better at my job—or so I thought—because I didn't have anyone to worry about. Unlike a lot of people who search for their past, I didn't feel lost. I felt free. But my mind has changed over the past few years, and since then what I've learned is… painful."

Sable turned onto her side, focused on his handsome profile. "Why?"

"My mother was a teenager when she had me, and she didn't want me." He spoke in a low voice meant to hide his emotions but instead magnified them.

Her chest hurt. His pain was palpable.

"How do you know that for sure?" Sable asked in a soft voice.

He glanced at her. "She met my father one summer, they had sex, and she left me with him and came back to France."

"Maybe there was a reason she did, Hunter. She left you with your *father*. Not a stranger."

"He died when I was almost a year old, and she never came to get me, Sable. I was put in the system."

"She might not have known," Sable said gently.

"You're being optimistic."

"I'm being objective, and positive, like you've encouraged me to be. It's not easy being a parent—loving a child and wanting the best for them—and half the time not knowing if the decisions you make *are* the best."

"Yeah well, when parents screw up, the kids are the ones who get hurt." He faced the ceiling again, his resentment at his mother not allowing him to see her as anything more than a woman who'd abandoned him because she didn't care.

Sable absorbed his anger and digested his words. "You said she passed away a few years after your father died. Do you have pictures or anything else of hers?"

"A few photos, and… my mother was a novelist."

"I remember you said that."

"Not a good one, apparently. She published a book at twenty-one, and it flopped. I've tried to find it, but... I don't know why I want to find that fucking book so bad." He ran an exasperated hand down his face.

She wanted to help him move past his anger and pain. "What's the title?"

Shooting a glance at her from the corner of his eye, Hunter asked, "You're not going to let this go, are you?"

"No."

He gave a short laugh and shook his head. "Hand me my wallet."

She picked it up from the bedside table and gave it to him.

He removed a photo from inside. "This is my mother. Amelie Sasson."

The woman in the photo had blond hair and light eyes.

"She's beautiful. You have her eyes."

"I have two more photos, but I left them at home." His voice remained emotionless, as if they were discussing which groceries to pick up from the market. From experience, Sable knew the harder a person tried to hide their feelings, the greater the emotions that lay beneath the surface.

Next, Hunter removed a folded piece of paper from the wallet. Rising onto her elbow, Sable watched as he opened the glossy sheet and showed her the picture of a book with the title, *Les fleurs d'amour* by Amelie Sasson.

"The flowers of love," she translated.

"Yeah. This is her novel. From what I've read online, it's a book about self-discovery. I've searched everywhere, but it's out of print." His voice sounded extra low and heavy from disappointment.

"Maybe I can help."

One eyebrow shot higher. "How?"

"Have you ever been along the Seine, where the booksellers sell used books?"

The *bouquinistes* were a fixture on the left and right banks of the Seine River. The tradition of peddling secondhand books started in the sixteenth century when vendors sold from wooden carts. Today, they rented green stalls that stretched for miles and sold not only used and rare books, but vintage magazines, postcards, and stamps. Whenever Sable visited Paris, she stopped by and browsed the selections, picking up souvenirs for herself, Avril, and their friends.

"I'm way ahead of you. I've been there, and I approached a few of the booksellers, but they aren't familiar with this novel. One thought he might know it and said he'd try to get me a copy. When I went back, he said he couldn't find any. Then I visited a couple of bookstores in the city. Nothing."

"Because you don't know who to ask, but I know someone who could probably find a copy of this book for you. His name is Robert, and he's a *bouquiniste*—one of the booksellers along the Seine. He can find anything, but it might cost you."

Hunter's eyes brightened. He'd feigned indifference to his mother but, like anyone else searching for their past, was interested in any tidbits of information available.

"I don't care how much it costs," he said.

"So you want me to reach out to him?" Sable asked.

His gaze dropped to the creased image of his mother's book. She understood his hesitation. It wasn't that he wasn't interested. He simply didn't want to get disappointed again. "Yes."

Sable pressed a comforting kiss to his shoulder. She desperately wanted him to have a piece of his history and would do anything she could to make it happen.

"Okay."

Lights flashed against Hunter's closed eyelids.

"What is that?" Sable muttered.

"I don't know," he grumbled, rolling over so he could burrow deeper under the covers. He pulled her closer. He desperately needed to sleep.

Sable moaned, snuggling into his arms.

Hunter's eyes cracked open, and he stiffened. Flashing blue light traipsed across the wall and ceiling of the dark bedroom. His heart jumpstarted, and he rolled away from Sable.

"Hey," she muttered, rubbing her eyes.

Hunter hurried to the window and peeked out. Six white police cars were parked on the street, their bright blue lights running across the walls of the buildings. Officers stood beside them, congregated together as if deciding their next move. Across the street, neighbors peered out the windows and watched the activity.

"Oh no." Though she couldn't see from the bed, Sable caught on.

"We need to leave," Hunter said.

When he turned away from the window, Sable was already on her feet, tugging on her underwear.

"How did they find us?"

"It was only a matter of time," he said, though certain they'd been ratted out by the guy who saw them coming into the building earlier.

He cursed softly. They had drawn attention to themselves.

They dressed in a rush, and then Sable grabbed the backpack. She pulled open one of the drawers to start loading in items, but Hunter grabbed her upper arm. "We don't have time. Let's go."

They raced toward the front door and Hunter yanked it open.

"How will we—" Sable gasped.

Six police officers stood outside, and as soon as the door opened, two of them lifted drawn weapons in their direction.

"Do not move!" one of the men said in a thick French accent.

"Hands in the air!" another yelled.

Hunter and Sable flung their hands up.

They were in deep trouble.

22

The police had separated them.

Sable sat in the living room with her hands cuffed behind her back. Hunter was in the bedroom with two officers, also handcuffed. The other officers had disappeared downstairs after Hunter and Sable's apprehension.

The investigating detective, dressed in plain clothes, was an older man with graying hair and a large mole on his right cheek. She recognized him from the newscast after the deaths at the cafe.

Gaspard Delon sat in front of her with a world weary expression, the kind someone wore when tired of witnessing the ugliness of humanity. He studied her in silence, legs crossed and one hand tapping a small notepad on his knee. She wondered what he was thinking. Was the silent treatment meant to throw her off-kilter and force a confession? He was wasting his time, because she wasn't guilty and really good at keeping her mouth shut if necessary.

"Veronica, you are in a lot of trouble." He spoke to her in English, using the alias from her fake passport.

Sable remained quiet, trying hard not to let fear swallow her whole.

"For someone so small, you are very dangerous and have caused a lot of problems." He set both feet on the floor and leaned forward, as if examining a particularly heinous-looking bug. "You killed Senator Richelieu."

Her heart jumped in her chest. "I did *not* kill the senator."

"We have statements from the security staff at Mr. Moreau's estate saying that's exactly what happened."

Sable leaned forward too, to get her point across. "*They're lying.*"

His resulting smile was condescending. "And why should I believe you?"

"Jean-Jacques Moreau is the one who killed Senator Richelieu. He's the real criminal."

"Mr. Moreau is a businessman. You broke into his home and robbed him, and when Senator Richelieu, at Mr. Moreau's home as a guest, discovered you, you killed him."

Sable's stomach burned with anxiety. "Not true! Mr. Moreau's security—"

"Bertrand Matisse was a member of the security staff who provided a statement about the events of the night in question. Conveniently, you and your boyfriend murdered him at the cafe."

"You can't really think we go around killing people? That was self-defense! He and his goons drove into the cafe to get us."

"Witnesses say they lost control of the vehicle—"

"Witnesses are lying!" Sable all but screamed, frustrated.

"Everyone is lying?"

"Bertrand and those other men tried to kill us, that's why they crashed into the restaurant, because it was faster and easier. Before they came after us, they murdered my friend, Michel, at his shop, Les Antiquités de Paris."

He appeared unmoved by her words and tapped the Gutenberg Bible on the table. "This belongs to Mr. Moreau. Do you deny taking it?"

Sable's lips tightened. She refused to incriminate herself.

"You and your boyfriend will have to pay for your crimes."

An officer came from the back. A scar ran from the corner of his mouth down his chin. He spoke to Delon in French. "We haven't found anything else except potential evidence of criminal behavior. Colored contacts, prosthetics, lock-picking tools. Things of that nature. According to his passport, the man's name is Hunter Miller." He held up Hunter's switchblade in an evidence bag. "And we found this."

Sable leveled her gaze at the floor. They didn't know she spoke French, and she intended to keep her secret for now.

"Perfect," Delon replied, also in French. "I'm sure that knife was used to commit other crimes, don't you think? We're done here."

Sable's breath snagged in her throat. Their conversation gave her a bad vibe.

"What does Philippe want us to do?" the officer with the scar asked.

Delon stood, and her eyes followed the movement. He picked up the Bible.

"He wants this mess cleaned up. No loose ends. We have everything we need. Make it look as if they were resisting arrest, which is easy enough to believe with these two. They're wanted for a total of five murders between them. I'll take the Bible downstairs and make sure no one comes up while you wrap up."

What the hell? They were planning to kill her and Hunter. No other explanation for what he said.

After Delon exited, the uniformed officer pinched Sable's arm in a tight grip and dragged her toward the bedroom. She stumbled at his rough handling, heart racing as she wondered what to do. He shoved her ahead of him through the door. The officer guarding Hunter was younger with dark hair.

"They're going to kill us!" Sable screamed for Hunter's benefit.

All three men were startled by her outburst, but Hunter recovered first and jumped into action. Hands locked behind his back, he charged the officer who had been in the room with him. The cop slammed backward into the wall under the weight of Hunter's powerful body. Scarface shoved Sable out of the way to aid his fellow officer.

As the men struggled, she flopped backward on the bed. Wiggling her butt, she shifted her hands under her legs and pulled her knees up to her chest to slip her handcuffed hands in front of her.

Hunter had managed to force both men to the floor with him in a tussle for life and death. He head butted the younger officer by flinging his head backward. His hard skull connected with the officer's face, and the back of his head bounced off the wall, knocking him unconscious, blood leaking from his nose.

Scarface staggered to his feet and reached for the gun in his holster. Thinking fast, Sable snatched the lamp from beside the bed and swung hard into the back of his head.

He yelped in pain and dropped to his knees within range of Hunter's foot. Hunter's heel planted a powerful blow to his jaw and sent him tumbling backward with blood spewing from his mouth.

The gun clattered to the floor and slid under the bed, and Sable scrambled for it. She grabbed the weapon and jumped to her feet, breathing in short anxious spurts as her pulse thumped erratically under her skin.

She pointed the muzzle at the older officer. She had never held a gun before, and it was a lot heavier than she expected. Her hands shook, but she held on tight.

Hunter moved to her side. "Get the handcuff keys off him."

He jerked his head in the direction of the knocked out officer behind them.

He then walked over to the one slouched against the wall. The man cowered, but Hunter didn't hit him again. He put his shoe to his neck. "Move and I'll crush your goddamn windpipe."

The man put a hand on Hunter's ankle, but otherwise he didn't move as he stared up at him.

"Detective Delon just left to take the Bible downstairs, but he's coming back." Sable lifted the keys and unlatched Hunter's handcuffs.

"We need to hurry then." He unlatched hers and carefully removed the weapon from her hand. "Get your things together."

While she stuffed items into the backpack, Hunter bound the wrists of the two officers together with one cuff and attached the second cuff to a foot of the bed. Then he kicked their radios out of reach.

Regaining consciousness, the younger officer groaned. He touched his face and winced, then stared in horror at the blood smeared on his fingers.

"You'll never get away with this. You are dead!" yelled the older officer.

Sable's heart shuddered to a stop, and she paused to look at him.

"I should blow a hole in your face for planning to murder us," Hunter said.

She didn't know if he was serious or not, but he sounded and looked grim-faced enough to carry out the threat. Moreau's reach clearly went deep into the depths of law enforcement. No wonder the last investigation into his warehouse went nowhere. One of his contacts must have tipped him off. How far did his tentacles go? She wasn't a violent person but couldn't fault Hunter if he pulled the trigger.

Sable stuffed as much as she could into the Army sack—phones, passports, and tools of the trade. Hunter then secured it to his back to keep his hands free.

"We can't go out the front," Sable said, pulling her hair into a hasty ponytail as he walked away from the officers.

"You're right. That's why we're going through the roof."

They rushed to the door, and Hunter flung it open. For the second time that night, they froze, and her heart plummeted.

On the other side, Detective Delon was reaching for the doorknob with two uniformed officers at his side.

T he detective reached for the gun in his hip holster, but Hunter was faster. He tapped the muzzle of the gun to the middle of the other man's forehead.

His trigger finger itched. "Move and I'll blow your fucking head off."

He hadn't expected Delon to return to the apartment so quickly. He'd thought they had more time.

No one moved. Not Delon. Not the two uniformed officers behind him. Not even Sable.

Delon gulped, hand frozen at his hip. "Can I lower my hand?"

"Slowly. And tell your men not to make any sudden moves."

The detective repeated the words in French and lowered his hand to his side. "What happened to my officers?"

"We took care of them. Lucky for you, I was feeling generous and didn't do to them what you planned to do to us, you son of a bitch. You working for Moreau?"

"I do not know what you mean."

"Yeah right."

"I speak fluent French. I heard what you told the officer to do. You planned to kill us," Sable said.

Delon narrowed his eyes at her and then returned his attention to Hunter. "No one will ever believe you. You must give up and spare yourself unnecessary pain."

"No thanks," Hunter said. "She's going to take your weapon, and you're going to let her. Go ahead, babe. Relieve the nice policeman of his Glock."

Delon stared at him with murderous eyes.

Sable took the gun and quickly stepped back.

"Toss it downstairs," he told her.

She did as he asked, and the gun hit the tile below with a loud clack.

"Anyone else armed?" Hunter knew better than to shift his gaze from the detective, who could quickly get the upper hand with them standing so close.

"The one behind him has a gun," Sable said.

"Tell him to toss it over the railing to the lower floor," Hunter said.

Delon repeated the command in French.

From his peripheral vision, Hunter saw the officer slowly unclip his holster and remove the weapon. He kept his eyes locked on Delon and the gun against his forehead, arm straight, finger on the trigger. The air was tight with tension. He'd have no qualms about blowing the detective's brains onto his fellow officers if he blinked wrong.

The officer tossed the weapon, and it dropped with a loud clatter to the floor below.

"Go upstairs, babe," Hunter said to Sable. "I'm right behind you."

Sable raced up the stairs, and when she had gone a safe distance, he slowly backed away from the cops.

"Don't even think about following," he said. Then he took off.

The men below yelled in French as he took the stairs two at a time. He arrived at the latched door where Sable was stalled. She couldn't get onto the roof.

"Stand back."

She stepped aside, and he fired one shot and blew off the lock. He shouldered open the heavy steel door, and they climbed out.

The rain had stopped, but the pitch of the roof would make traveling across it dangerous.

"Careful," he warned.

Sable was adept at scaling multi-story walls and slipping undetected into homes, but he still worried about her safety.

Voices came up the stairs behind them, and they didn't stick around to see who was coming. They raced across the rooftop.

"They're not going to stop," Sable said.

"That's why we need to keep going."

A shot cracked in the night air. They both ducked, and Hunter shoved Sable behind an air conditioner fan.

"Stay low," he said.

"Okay." Her voice was soft and breathless.

Hunter took a quick look in the direction they'd come from. In the dark it was hard to see, but he could tell the door was ajar. Delon popped his head and half his body from behind the steel and fired another shot. The bullet went wide, and Sable let out a noncommittal sound, cowering behind the unit with her hands over her ears. The detective slipped out of sight again to protect himself from return fire.

As a sharpshooter, Hunter had the greatest accuracy of his team at the agency, so he became hyper focused. He hugged the AC and lined up the shot with one hand. When the detective popped out and fired another shot, Hunter didn't flinch. He simply pulled the trigger.

The bullet connected. Delon yelled in pain and dropped his

gun. Hunter fired again. The warning shot forced Delon to slam the door closed.

"Go!"

They took off across the rooftop and jumped to the next building. They did the same two more times, but the second time Sable slipped on the landing. He caught her arm and yanked her upright so they could keep running. Every now and again, they skidded on the rain-slick surfaces but maintained their balance.

With a running start, they vaulted across the open space toward the fourth building and landed with soft knees. Hunter hit first with a grunt, and Sable was right behind him. They ran over to the edge of the building and looked back. No one behind them.

"We'll go down here. Can you do it?" He pointed at the metal downspout attached to the building.

"In my sleep," Sable replied.

Other than fellow agents, he'd never met a woman as skilled and adventurous as she was. He grabbed the back of her neck and kissed her hard. "Damn, you're sexy."

She grinned. His chest tightened, and his whole world shifted. He didn't want to think about these feelings for her. His reaction could be caused by the adrenaline pumping through his veins. He hoped so, or he was in deep trouble.

Hunter threw his legs over the side of the roof and slid down the metal downspout. Sable followed behind him, landing lightly on her feet. Tennis shoes slapping the cobblestone beneath their feet, they ran along a backstreet with few pedestrians and ignored the curious looks directed their way.

Finally, they stopped to rest in the doorway of a boutique. Chests heaving, they slipped into the shadows and away from the street lights.

As soon as he caught his breath, Hunter dialed Hossam's number, but the call went to voicemail.

"Shit."

Almost immediately, Hossam's number popped up on the return call.

"Hossam."

"I was about to call you," his friend whispered. "I was hauled into a meeting by my old supervisors. They demanded to know if I knew I was harboring fugitives at my apartment. I told them I barely knew you and didn't know about your criminal background. Otherwise, they would have arrested me. They're now questioning the validity of the photos you sent. Where are you?"

Dammit. Bad news about the photos.

Hunter's eyes surveyed the street. "I'm not sure where we are. We took off on foot and ran as fast as we could. Hossam, we can't trust the police. Gaspard Delon, the investigating officer, was going to kill us tonight. He's on Moreau's payroll."

"What! I know Gaspard. Are you sure?"

"Yes. We need your help. We need someplace to lie low."

Hossam muttered something in Arabic. "Okay, let me think." He fell silent. "I have an idea. Can you stay out of sight for another hour? It might not be that long, but I need to see if any of the safe houses in inventory are unoccupied. If so, you can stay at one of them."

"Do what you need to do. We can stay out of sight."

"Good. I'll be in touch."

After the call ended, Sable touched Hunter's arm.

"What did he say?"

"He's going to find us a place. A safe house, but he has to make sure it's unoccupied. Until then, we need to stay out of sight."

The sound of screaming sirens traveled down another street, and Sable shivered.

Hunter took her hand and led her behind some buildings into an empty courtyard. They sat in the shadows on the damp cement, and Hunter placed an arm around her shoulders.

"This has got to be the longest night of my life." Sable snuggled closer and rested her head on his shoulder. "Change of plans, by the way. I'm not sure I want to go into the antiques business after all."

Hunter laughed and kissed the top of her head. At least she still had her sense of humor.

"Stay away from money launderers and drug traffickers, and you should be fine."

They waited in the dark for almost forty-five minutes. At first, they heard police sirens every five minutes. Each time, Sable squeezed closer to him. Then all they heard were the distant sounds of cars going by and the occasional laughter of people walking the street at the front of the buildings.

The phone buzzed. Hossam.

"Where are you?" his friend asked.

Hunter gave him the cross streets.

"I know exactly where you are. I'll be there in less than thirty minutes."

They hung up, and he and Sable waited.

When Hossam arrived, they climbed into the car and hunkered down in the backseat.

"It's going to be awhile. We're going outside the city to a secluded area."

Hunter appreciated the information about the location. Safe houses in the city were convenient, but he preferred the ones outside the city. Better privacy and less chance of detection because there weren't nosy neighbors close by.

They stayed low until Hossam told them, "You can sit up now. We're off the highway."

There were few lights on the road they traveled. Eventually, they pulled up to a gate. Hossam hopped out and opened it and drove in. He locked it back before taking a winding driveway to a dark, wood frame house at the end. He pulled up to door, and they all climbed out.

"This way."

Hossam entered a code and let them inside, switching on an overhead light. They walked deeper into a house furnished with modern decor—like a suite at a high end hotel—beneath fourteen-foot vaulted ceilings.

"There's a security room with monitors that way, but they're turned off now. Don't turn them on, or it'll send a signal and alert the network someone is here. This will be your home for now. During the day, you can see a small lake out the window there. The door automatically locks when you exit through the front or back. The code at the back is 5463. The code for the front door is 7980. There's a car in the garage you can use. Keys are in the bowl over there. There isn't much food here except canned goods. I can give you some cash until—"

"I have my wallet," Hunter interrupted.

"Good. If you go back down the road we came in on and turn right, a few miles down is a market where they sell fresh produce."

"How long can we stay here?" Hunter placed the backpack on the sofa facing the picture window.

"Unfortunately, you're not here in an official capacity. A week maybe, assuming no one needs the space before then."

He looked contrite, and Hunter didn't want him feeling guilty about something he had no control over. He'd be in enough trouble dealing with the fallout of harboring fugitives in his apartment. Hunter knew how the government worked. They were not done giving Hossam a hard time, and he'd have to be extra careful moving forward because he'd have eyes on him.

"Thank you for your help." Hunter clapped his friend on the shoulder.

"You would do the same for me."

"I'm sorry I've caused so much trouble," Sable said.

"Do not say that," Hossam chided her. He squeezed her arm. "If I could, I would get you out of this with the snap of a finger."

They all sat down on chairs in the room, and Hunter and Sable gave him a rundown of the night's events, including more details about the warehouse. Hossam listened with a deep frown, every now and again interjecting with questions.

"We need to put a stop to this man and clear your names."

"But how?" Sable asked.

Hunter didn't have the answer right then, but he intended to find a way.

24

oments later, they were all sipping coffee as they discussed options. Sable in an armchair with her legs folded beneath her while Hossam sat on the sofa, and Hunter paced the room with a mug in his hand.

Sable cradled her cup and took another sip of coffee, grateful for its warmth flushing the chill of the damp night out of her bones.

"Moreau must have a second set of books. There's always a second set of books with the accurate financials. We just have to figure out where they are," Hunter said.

He stopped in front of the fireplace and drank from his mug. In deep concentration and frowning, his fierce expression sent a thrill through Sable.

"They could be at his office, but we'd have to find a way in. Or they could be at his home. They could be anywhere," Hossam said. "Still doesn't get your names cleared of the murders."

Hunter halted his movements. "The video! They shared a video of Sable the night of the news broadcast."

Sable dropped her bare feet to the floor. "Right, the video

from Moreau's office. If we get our hands on the entire video—not the edited one Moreau provided, we could prove he and Bertrand lied, and *they* killed the senator. And I think I know where the video backup is. When I broke into Moreau's office, I saw a hard drive in the safe. I didn't pay it much attention, but what if there's a backup of the video on the drive?"

Hossam slowly nodded. "Who knows what else could be on there. Maybe the second set of financials proving he's doctoring the books."

"We need to get back into his office and the safe," Hunter said.

"I could break in again," Sable offered.

Neither man looked enthusiastic about her idea, shooting uneasy glances at each other.

"His security will be at a higher level now. We'd have to stake out the house to find a way in," Hunter remarked.

"Or," Hossam said, a smile on his face. "You crash the party he's having next weekend. I was going to give you a full update when we talked, but Moreau and his wife are having a big cocktail party. Some of her old Hollywood friends will be in attendance, and Moreau has also invited business associates. The party is being billed as a celebration of his company's success. The five-year anniversary of turning things around. It's expected to be a huge formal event, and from what I understand, several politicians will be in attendance."

"I wonder if a certain detective will be there," Sable mumbled bitterly.

Hunter resumed pacing. "So we find a way into the party, and Sable gets into the safe again and swipes the external drive."

"How do we get you into the party on such short notice? Maybe as members of the catering staff? No, that wouldn't work." Hossam shook his head in disgust and flopped against the back of the sofa.

Hunter stopped moving and grinned. "What if we can get an invitation? We don't have a lot of time, but it's possible. We'd have to go through the weakest link."

Hossam sat up. "What are you thinking?"

"Who's the weakest link?" Sable asked, thoroughly confused.

"The wealth manager," Hunter answered. "To stop Moreau, we're going to have to go through him."

"How?"

"We become one of his clients. We become drug dealers who need to launder money."

A smile broke out on Hossam's face. "Become a client and get an invite to meet the man in charge."

"Exactly."

Hossam glanced at his watch and swore softly. "I've been gone long enough and need to get back. I've talked to my contacts about the police raiding the warehouse, but they're hesitant. Moreau has probably moved everything by now, but I'm pushing as hard as I can."

"Go. I'll work on a plan and reach out to you later," Hunter said.

Hossam shook his head. "I have to stop communicating with you on this phone for a while. I'm sure my former employers will start monitoring my calls, if they haven't already. When I get back to Paris, I'll purchase a burner phone so we can stay in touch."

"Sounds good."

Hossam stood and Sable came to her feet.

"Thank you for everything." She pulled him into a warm hug.

He kissed her temple. "Take care of my friend," he said over her shoulder to Hunter.

"I will."

"He's taking good care of me," Sable assured him.

Hossam picked up his keys. "I'll be in touch tomorrow. Get some rest you two."

Hunter walked him to the door. When he came back, he pulled Sable into his arms, and she wrapped hers around his waist.

"You ready to go to sleep? I desperately need some sleep," she said.

"I need to make a call first. You go to bed."

"Are you going to tell me what you're up to?"

"I will, but I'm working on the idea and need to talk to someone who knows more than I do. I have to make a call to my agency. We're going to need reinforcements."

"Okay." She trusted him completely. Rising on her toes, she kissed his mouth.

He groaned and palmed her butt.

Laughing, Sable looped her arms around his neck and indulged in a more thorough kiss. When she withdrew, she gazed into his gray eyes. They were soft as he looked down at her, his lips curled in a smile.

The relentless butterflies in her stomach made her suddenly become emotional, thinking about what would happen if they managed to get the goods on Moreau and clear their names. She and Hunter had just gone with the flow, but she couldn't ignore the swirl of emotions taking hold inside of her. Perhaps being in constant contact with him and almost losing her life several times was clouding her judgment, but she almost believed she was falling for him.

She dropped her gaze, afraid he'd see the truth. "Good night."

"Good night, babe."

Babe. All of a sudden he started using the endearment, and she liked the intimacy the word suggested.

She left him alone in the living room and went up to bed.

HUNTER SAT on the sofa and listened to the phone ringing in the States.

"Hello?" Cruz Cordoba, the owner of The Cordoba Agency, answered on the third ring.

Hunter met the Cuban immigrant when they both worked for Plan B. Cruz was the best all-around agent he'd ever met. Smart as hell, great in hand-to-hand combat, and a dangerous killing machine.

Although Hunter initially expressed uncertainty about working for his agency, he was now glad he'd accepted Cruz's offer. Being around him, his family, and the rest of the agents—whom Hunter considered family—had been the main reason he'd finally pursued the research into his background.

"Cruz, I hate to bother you at home, but I'm in deep shit here in France."

"Who's that?" a female voice asked. His wife, Shanice.

"Hunter. I'll take the call in my office."

Hunter heard rustling as Cruz apparently climbed out of bed and left their bedroom.

"What's going on?" his friend asked.

"I'm wanted as an accomplice to murder."

"How did that happen? I thought you were on vacation."

He laughed and rubbed the back of his neck as he walked the length of the room. "My trip turned into much more than a vacation. I'm still sorting through the plans in my head, but I'm going to need help."

He launched into an explanation and Cruz listened, helping him fix the holes in the plan to make the execution solid and less likely to fail.

"I wish I could be there with you, but Shanice is having a tough time with this pregnancy. Her mother is here, but I don't want to leave her."

"I understand, and you shouldn't. Who can you spare?" Hunter asked.

"Do you need comms?"

"No. I'm pretty sure I can get everything I need through Hossam."

"Alissa planned to go to the Virgin Islands but hasn't left yet, so she's free."

"What about Sanchez?" He would be an integral part of the plan.

"I can pull him from a low priority job and send him over," Cruz said.

"Great, thanks." Everything was falling into place.

"Anything else?"

"Not that I can think of."

"Get this cleared up. We need you back here."

"I plan to. I have no doubt I can get us out of the country, but I don't want to be looking over my shoulder for the rest of my life, and I don't want that for Sable. When we leave France, we leave with our names cleared."

"You think of anything else you need, let me know," Cruz said.

"I will." Hunter hung up the phone in much better spirits than when he called.

He went upstairs and eased open the door of the master bedroom. In the quiet room, Sable lay on her side in the dark, navy sheets pulled up to her neck.

Hunter undressed and climbed into bed. Lying on his back, he stared up at the ceiling, hands linked behind his head.

Sable rolled toward him and placed one smooth leg across his, her soft breasts mashed against his side. She was naked, and his body started hardening at the contact.

"Did I wake you?" He dropped an arm around her.

"I heard you come in. I've been waiting for you to come to bed."

He liked the way she said that, as if joining her in bed was a normal occurrence. A thought blipped across his brain of how sharing a bed with her *could* become a normal occurrence—one he would look forward to and enjoy.

She ran her hands over the hairs on his chest and played with his nipple. "Did you figure things out?"

"Yeah." He could barely concentrate with her touching him. His semi-hard erection would turn into a steel rod if she kept that up. "Help is on the way."

He pulled her hair loose of the ponytail, and as he massaged her scalp, she moaned.

"Are you sure you're ready for what's to come?"

"I'm ready for anything with you," she whispered.

His gut tightened.

He rolled her onto her back and gave her an intense kiss, one filled with longing and hunger and promises he couldn't yet articulate. His finger raked through her soft hair and gripped a handful, tilting back her head for a breath-stealing, passionate kiss.

She made mewling sounds as he sucked on her neck and groaned aloud when he kissed her breasts and sucked her dark nipples. The urge to plunge into her right away was overwhelming, but he wanted more time to enjoy her sexy body. Kissing and sucking. Licking and touching. She smelled good. She tasted good. And the way she moved... *goddamn.*

"*Hunter*," she moaned, her voice hard as if she were angry at him.

She was wet and horny and writhing out of control. Her enthusiasm weakened his resolve, and he was so anxious to get inside her, he almost forgot to use protection. Hunter retrieved a condom from his wallet and slipped it on fast. Then he held his thick length in hand before sliding between her spread legs.

Back arching off the bed, she let out a wail of pleasure. The sound sent warm tingles across his back. Propped up on his hands, Hunter looked down at her with a rigid jaw as he worked hard to make her feel good—to make her feel even a semblance of how he did inside her.

"Yeah—oh, yes." Her voice shook, and she reached for him, dragging his body on top of hers.

Their kiss was hungry and greedy and out of control. When the dam broke, Sable clawed his back. She tried to control the movement by increasing the tempo of the thrusts, but he maintained a steady rhythm—long and slow as if he owned all the time in the world.

He locked her wrists above her head with one hand and continued to work his hips, determined to give her another shattering release before he took his.

Voice pleading, Sable whimpered his name, which only made him go harder, more determined to please her.

"Fuck your little friend in Nashville. I'ma make sure you *never* forget this dick," he growled.

He squeezed her breast, and she came again. Gasping, mouth falling open, her body rocking and jerking from the intensity of her orgasm.

Hunter's toes curled tight as he tried to prolong the wait to his own climax, but those feminine muscles quivering around him for a second time were too much.

"Goddamn," he whispered.

His fingers squeezing her delicate wrists as his tight control unraveled.

"*God. Damn.*"

He jackhammered inside her as his body emptied. The only other time he'd nutted so hard and good was hours ago, last time he was inside her.

He groaned aloud and collapsed on his side, dragging her with him. Cradling the back of her head with one palm, harsh breaths burst from his mouth as they curled around each other.

Eyes squeezed shut, his throat tightened with emotion.

Whatever he was feeling, he'd never experienced it before. Possessive anger. Jealousy of an invisible man.

This woman and all the moments they'd spent together rushed through his brain. Cooking together, laughing together, dodging bullets together, making love. He'd opened up to her in a way he hadn't to many other people.

Too bad they were in their current predicament. Otherwise, they could make an attempt to have a real relationship. Instead, they were stuck hiding in a safe house.

Being with her in their current situation wasn't perfect by any means, but it was still good.

Almost perfect.

25

S able stayed at the house while Hunter went to the market to pick up groceries. After the night they'd had, exhaustion kept her in bed. He didn't need as much sleep as she did and left early.

When she finally went downstairs, she did yoga on the patio in front of the lake, listening to chirping birds and watching tiny frogs hop through the grass. She hadn't been able to exercise for a while, and as she stretched and curved her body into the different poses, the concerns of the last few days temporarily disappeared.

By the end of the session, with a centered mind and loose muscles, she padded into the kitchen and poured a cup of coffee from the pot Hunter brewed before he left. She spent the rest of the morning searching the news online. No mention of the break-in at the warehouse, but a reporter interviewed Detective Delon about the escaped fugitives and the resulting shootout, which caused him to have an injured hand wrapped in a bandage.

When Hunter returned later, he came in with a bunch of bags and made two trips to bring in everything.

"What did you buy?" she asked, following him into the kitchen.

"Mostly meat, chicken, fruit, and veggies," he replied.

Sable held up a bag of sweet potato chips and two candy bars. "And these?"

Hunter shrugged, placing rice and pasta in the cabinets. "We'll need those snacks when my friends arrive."

Sable shook her head. He had such a big appetite. "These are for you, and you'll probably eat all of them before they arrive," she teased.

He swatted her behind, and she laughed. "Stop!"

They finished putting away the food, which included more chips, candy, and other snacks than she originally noticed.

Then Hunter pulled her against him and kissed her nose. "Come here. I brought you something." Taking her hand, he led her to the living room, where he'd placed several bags.

"What's all this?"

"Open those two. They're yours."

Inside were clothes and underwear. She held up two black thongs. "Really?"

He gave his most innocent look. "What? You don't like them?"

She shook her head at him. "Yes, I like them, and they're my size."

"I know."

Sable stuffed the clothes back in the bag and walked over to him. "Thank you."

He pulled her onto his lap. "You're welcome."

She kissed him gently, affectionately, savoring the firmness of his mouth. "How is your arm?"

"Fine. I put on a new bandage before I left to go shopping." He stretched out his arm to show her how well he was doing.

Sable ran her fingertips over the bandage. "Do you think we'll really be able to take down Moreau and his accomplices?"

"Definitely. If we get the full video, he's done."

"I hope so. He needs to pay for his crimes—not only for what he did to the senator, but for what he did to Michel." She shivered at the memory of her dead friend in the chair at his antique shop.

"How long have you known Michel?" Hunter asked.

"A few years. I met him through another thief named Gene. Older white guy. He's retired now but always dresses sharp. I used to go to the library to use the computer because I couldn't afford to pay for Wi-Fi in the boarding house where I lived with my daughter. I hated that room, but it was all I could afford."

She fell into introspective silence, recalling the cramped quarters and having to share a bed with a child whose poor sleeping habits meant getting kicked and slapped throughout the night.

"What about your daughter's father?"

Sable gave a short laugh. She wanted to open up but needed a little more distance between them. She slipped off Hunter's lap but kept her legs thrown across his thighs. Without saying a word, he stroked her lower leg, gently encouraging her to talk.

Sable kept her gaze dipped to her intertwined fingers. "Avril's father is um... Southern royalty, so to speak. I spent the first three years of her life trying to force a paternity test, but his parents have a lot of money, and they delayed and delayed to protect their son. They refused to acknowledge my relationship with Andrew, much less that Avril is his daughter. Turns out I wasn't his only 'girlfriend.' At that young age, he'd already mastered the art of lying and juggling multiple women. I can't believe I was ever stupid enough to believe he loved me."

His hand stopped moving. "I'm sorry."

She shrugged dismissively. "We do okay without him."

"But you didn't always," he said matter-of-factly.

"No." She lifted her gaze to Hunter's. "What I do now is a far cry from who I used to be. The old me shoplifted by hiding diapers in my daughter's stroller and hid loaves of bread inside my winter coat. I used to pickpocket too, and one of my hunting grounds was the library, if you can believe that. I used the computer but also checked out books—for Avril and for me. I picked stories I could sign to her at bedtime, but me—I preferred nonfiction, specifically, history. I read everything I could get my hands on, which is why I fell in love with old objects and became interested in antiques."

"So how did you go from picking pockets to stealing from the bad guys, as you said?"

She grimaced in embarrassment. "Gene. About ten years ago he caught me lifting a woman's wallet from her purse, which was on the floor beside a desk, just sitting in the open. Extremely careless of her. Gene saw me and came toward me, and I held my breath, certain he'd rat me out. I had Avril with me, so I was terrified. I could lose my kid! He passed me by, but as he passed, he said, 'Follow me.' I don't know why I did."

She let out a little a laugh of disbelief. "I'm glad I did. While Avril ran around the playground, he and I talked. He told me there was another way—a network of thieves who took from criminals and disbursed the goods to the needy or their rightful owners."

"Sort of like Robin Hood?" Hunter asked, frowning.

She smiled briefly. "Sort of. Anyway, I trained with Gene for a year before he offered me my first job in Atlanta—a socialite's diamond necklace. She claimed it was stolen so her ex-husband couldn't have it as ordered in their divorce decree. I left Avril with my cousin—a single mom herself with three kids of her own—but I was desperate.

"I was gone for two days, and when I came back, I paid my cousin for taking care of Avril and had enough money to cover my expenses for *two* months!"

Over the years, those finder's fees paid for her and Avril to live a comfortable life. She couldn't afford to give her daughter the life her father could have, but she did her best to get close. Ballet classes, the occasional vacation, pricey gifts for her birthday and Christmas, and now college.

In addition to providing a better life, she prepared her daughter for adulthood. Her parents hadn't taught her much in terms of basic survival skills. Everything she'd learned, she learned on her own, out of necessity. How to cook, how to clean, how to budget. She made sure Avril learned those skills at an early age so she wouldn't be a late starter like Sable.

"I didn't only care about the money, you know? The jobs gave me a purpose. I wasn't only a thief—I was *helping* people."

"You've been through a lot," Hunter said in a grave voice.

She saw pity in his eyes. The emotion used to irritate her. She didn't like people feeling sorry for her but understood his concern.

"We're good now."

A thoughtful expression came into Hunter's eyes. "Sable—"

The phone in his pocket rang, cutting off what he was about to say. He checked the screen before answering. "I don't recognize the number. Must be Hossam on the new phone." He answered on speaker.

"I wish I could share better news, but law enforcement finally obtained a warrant to search the warehouse. All they found were offices and antiques. No money. The entire basement floor was empty."

"Dammit," Hunter said.

Sable's shoulder's drooped. "What now?"

"We have to find the external drive," Hossam said. "Whatever is on it—videos, financials, conversations—everything could be relevant. Moreau is old school and likes to have backup, as we saw with the information he wrote in invisible ink in the Bible. I have to believe the evidence to take down his empire and prove your innocence is on that disk. Otherwise..."

Sable swallowed. *Otherwise*, she was in a lot of trouble. Traveling on a fake passport and breaking into Moreau's office made her look capable of committing more heinous crimes.

"Thanks for the update, Hossam," Hunter said, though he didn't sound grateful. He sounded as disappointed as she was.

"I know this news is not what you wanted to hear, but that's all I have for now."

"Yeah, I know. Look, Alissa and Sanchez are flying over and should be here by this afternoon. Can you come back to the safe house to review the plan? We'll need your help."

"I'll be there, and I'll make a call to the bank like I promised. I'll give you an update when I get there."

"Great. Later."

They hung up, and Sable slipped from the sofa and walked over to the window overlooking the lake. Under different circumstances she would enjoy the lovely view.

"What are you thinking?" Hunter asked.

"I thought we were close, and I'm trying not to be negative, but everything hinges on the drive." Hands on her hips, she turned to face Hunter. "What if there's nothing on the drive? No video, no financials—nothing?"

Hunter crossed the room and placed his hands on her waist. "Then we keep trying. We can't give up. We'll get this guy."

Sable looked deeply into his eyes. She'd become so dependent on Hunter's strength and positive energy. "You sure?"

That was an unfair question, but she needed to believe they would stop Moreau.

"One hundred percent certain," he said.

26

B y midafternoon, Hunter's coworkers arrived with their bags in tow.

Sanchez and Alissa exuded an air of capability and no-nonsense about them, while at the same time coming off as friendly.

Alissa was a lovely Caribbean woman with blemish-free dark skin.

"It's nice to have another woman here," Sable said, shaking her hand.

"Nice to meet you," Alissa said, smiling.

Alejandro Sanchez, or Sanchez—as Hunter referred to him —was Mexican, with neck tattoos and a roguish grin. He kissed the back of her hand.

"Pleasure to meet you," he said, a gleam in his dark eyes.

"Enough of that," Hunter said, separating their hands and stepping between them.

After a hearty laugh, the four of them crowded around the table. Light coming in through the bay window illuminated the dining room, giving the space a bright, open feel.

Sable spread her fingers on the table. "I hate to sound naïve, but can someone please explain to me how this money laundering scheme works?"

Before anyone could answer, they heard the door open, and all heads turned in the direction of the noise. Hossam appeared in the doorway.

"Hello, everyone," he said, but his eyes landed on Alissa and stayed there.

"Hi, Hossam. You know Alissa. This is Alejandro Sanchez," Hunter said.

"I've heard a lot about you," Hossam said, extending a hand to the Mexican. Then he leaned across the table and extended a hand to Alissa, and his voice dropped. "Alissa, it's been a while."

She visibly stiffened. "It has." She took his hand but obviously didn't want to.

When Alissa tried to pull her arm back, he held on, a smile crossing his lips as they locked eyes. If looks could sever a human body, she would have sliced him in half.

Hunter cleared his throat and looked pointedly at Hossam. "I was about to explain the money laundering scheme to Sable."

Hossam released Alissa and sat in the chair directly across from her. "Don't let me interrupt you."

With one final glance at Hossam, Hunter continued. "Money laundering is taking illegally earned money and making it seem as if it comes from a legitimate source," he explained.

"I understand that part, but how is Moreau laundering the money?"

"Through the antique shops. His drivers collect the cash from Elan Crimini, and Moreau creates fake invoices to show his business is making more money than it really is. Some of the funds are deposited into his legitimate business accounts, and the rest is deposited into fake business accounts that really belong to Crimini, the ones listed in the Bible. Costas then invests the money into legitimate assets—mutual funds, art, other businesses, real estate, you name it."

"The financial crimes department is still digging, but I expect the assets are owned by shell companies connected to Crimini, who can then gradually make withdrawals over time by having the companies write checks to him, cashing out funds, or selling an asset," Hossam interjected.

"At that point, the money is washed?" Sable asked.

"Yes," Hunter said.

"It takes time to peel back the layers. These guys are good. None of the paperwork will show Crimini's name. Only lawyers and maybe business associates," Hossam said.

"Got it," she said.

"Anyone else find it odd they're laundering money through antique shops?" Alissa asked, looking around the table. "The businesses these people use to launder money tend to be a specific kind of high volume cash business—casinos, laundromats, restaurants."

"I'm convinced Crimini chose to work with Moreau for that very reason. The business is unconventional, unexpected," Hossam said. "Also, Moreau experienced financial difficulty years ago for selling fake antiques. Crimini knew he needed the money and recognized he would be working with someone with the same lack of morals."

"So my next question is, Hunter, how are you going to make sure you get invited to the party next weekend?" Sable asked. "Why would the wealth manager be interested?"

"Because these people only care about the bottom line," Hunter answered. "The more money deposited in the bank, the better. Typically, this type of activity goes all the way to the top. Costas has a boss who knows exactly what he's doing and doesn't care. Costas doesn't care, as long as he gets paid. A new player means more money for everyone involved. All we have to do is dangle a carrot in front of the greedy son of a bitch, and I guarantee he'll race to grab it.

"We're going to create a persona for Sanchez. A well-connected Colombian drug lord looking for a way to legitimize his money. Costas is used to dealing with wealthy, shady characters. All we have to do is make Sanchez appear to be a new player and get him to introduce Sanchez to Moreau."

"I made the call, and he has an appointment with Costas in three days," Hossam interjected.

"Excellent. Gives us enough time to finalize the details and pull together supplies and tech for the job. Three of us are going to the bank. The drug trafficker, his bodyguard, and his accountant."

"So Sanchez is the drug trafficker. Who's the bodyguard?" Sable asked.

"Me," Hunter answered.

"And the accountant?"

"You."

Her eyes widened. "Me?"

"Yes, and I'm turning you into a man for our scam."

THE NEXT MORNING, Sable made a big breakfast of potatoes, eggs, and macerated strawberries for the pancakes.

Hossam was back and brought a laptop on which was a floor plan of Moreau's estate. While he, Alissa, and Sanchez finalized details in the dining room, Sable and Hunter worked on getting her ready in the living room.

"I don't think this is going to work. You can't turn me into a man." Sable placed her hands on her hips. "Have you seen me?"

Hunter's eyes narrowed, and he licked his bottom lip. "Yeah, I've seen you *and* tasted you," he said in a lowered voice, and she blushed. "But don't worry, once I work my magic, no one is going to believe you're a woman. With the right wig, makeup, and clothes, I'll turn you into a nerdy little accountant."

"Not all accountants are nerdy. Or little, for that matter."

"You will be."

"You're serious."

"As a heart attack."

"Why not make me a female accountant?"

"Because the best disguises are in the opposite direction of your normal appearance. A woman with light hair should go dark and vice versa. A young person could be turned into an older person. You'll be turned into a man. But first, we need to make sure you're believable as a man. Let me see you walk across the room, the way a confident man would."

"I can walk like man," Sable said, slightly offended. She'd run plenty of scams in her time. Granted, she'd never pretended to be a man, but how hard could it be?

"Let. Me. See."

His tone of voice made her core throb. Hunter Miller was a danger to her libido.

She turned her back to him.

"Shoulders back," Hunter said.

She tossed a glare over her shoulder. "I know how to walk."

He folded his arms over his chest, a faint smile lifting the left corner of his mouth.

Sable started across the floor, bopping with the confidence of an imaginary man.

"Stop."

Annoyed, she swung to face Hunter. "I've only taken a few steps."

He pressed his fingertips to the bridge of his nose. "What the...? Are you a pimp?"

"I'm a confident man with swagger," she said, definitely offended now.

He bit his bottom lip, as if biting back tart words. "Could you do it without the swagger? Please."

"You sure? I could cut back—"

"No swagger. Walk like a normal man who doesn't have hoes."

Sable let out an exaggerated sigh and cut her eyes at him. She didn't think her walk was *that* bad.

She continued across the floor. At the far wall, she turned and came back toward Hunter, flinging her arms wide. "Ta-dah. Easy peasy."

"Way too much hip action. That's not how men walk."

"Some men do."

"Yeah, some gay men. But you're not gay, so that's not going to work."

"Why can't I be a gay man?"

"No." Hunter cupped her shoulders, his warm, firm hands spreading heat on her skin.

Turning her to face the far wall, he then stood beside her. "You have to become a man and think like a man. Women walk with their feet closer together, one foot in front of the other, which causes more hip motion. Men walk with their feet farther apart and take up more space because we tend to move our shoulders and arms more, *not* our hips. We also take longer strides. Watch me."

He walked across the carpeted floor, shoulders straight and head high. He moved with grace and style, but there was no mistaking him for a woman. At the end, he turned and walked back to her, and she paid attention—wide legs, longer strides.

"See the difference?" he asked.

"I think so."

"Now you try."

Sable rolled her shoulders, as if preparing for exercise, and then started to walk.

"Keep those feet apart," Hunter directed.

She corrected and kept moving, right away noticing a difference in her movement. She felt bigger, stronger, wider, and he was right, her arms swung more. As she returned to him, he was nodding, a smile of satisfaction on his face.

"Well?" He arched an eyebrow.

"You're right. There is a difference."

"Go back to your normal walk."

She did, and immediately noticed the difference in her body, the way her hips moved more. She felt more feminine with the smaller steps, one foot in front of the other.

She returned to him, shaking her head. "Wow, I had no idea…"

"Being in disguise isn't only about your clothes and makeup. It's how you carry yourself and the subtle differences that make each person who they are. There are cultural differences, whether you want to incorporate a limp when you walk, or a lisp when you talk. All of that is part of the equation when you're in disguise."

He was giving her a masterclass in subterfuge.

"Let me practice a little more. I want to get this."

She spent the next few minutes practicing the walk while Hunter looked on, every now and then interjecting a critique on ways to improve. When they finished, she was fairly confident.

"What about my physical appearance? What do you have in mind?"

"You'll need to remove your nail polish, and we can bind *them* down," he said, hands hovering in front of her breasts.

Sable's nipples tightened, and she was tempted to lean into his touch.

He gave her body a once-over. "And this," he continued, using his hands to make the shape of an hourglass. "Will be hidden under a suit."

Sable turned around. Looking over her shoulder at him, she

grabbed both of her ass cheeks. "What about this?" she asked, batting her eyelashes.

He laughed softly, his voice a little husky. "*Definitely* a problem, but I think I can figure out what to do with that ass."

She faced him and tilted her head up. "Just making sure."

"Uh-huh." Hunter stepped into her personal space. "I appreciate the concern and the dedication."

"I want everything to go well."

"So do I." He became serious all of a sudden. "I want you to be safe."

"I've been in way more dangerous situations than walking into a bank, Hunter. Besides, I trust you. I know nothing will happen to me while I'm with you."

Her chest tightened. Those weren't just words. She meant them. Without a doubt, whenever she was with this man, no harm would come to her, and accepting that truth was a revelation. Considering she'd been on her own for so long—she and Avril struggling to make ends meet until she accepted her ability as a thief—it was strange to think of someone else caring so much about her wellbeing.

Hunter stirred unfamiliar feelings within her. He was the kind of man who took care of his own, and she wanted to be *his*.

His smoldering gaze locked onto her mouth and sent a charge of heat coursing through her. She craved him. Badly, like some ravenous beast that hadn't eaten in decades. They had company, so she needed to behave.

But tonight, she would demonstrate just how much she craved him.

27

Banque Quotidienne was located in La Défense, a business district a couple of miles outside of Paris. The city contained cobblestoned streets and Haussmann-style buildings with mansard roofs and stone facades. By contrast, La Défense was modern, with skyscrapers and multi-story buildings made of glass and steel.

Acting as chauffeur and bodyguard, Hunter drove a Mercedes slowly toward their destination with Sanchez and Sable in the back. He cruised down the streets, scoping out the area behind dark sunglasses, his body fitted in an espresso suit and terra-cotta tie.

In addition to the sunglasses, he'd obscured his features with a goatee, prosthetic nose, and a black wig that gave him wavy hair overdue for a haircut. The strands swept across his forehead, curled around his ears, and touched the collar of his shirt.

He drove past the massive, cube-shaped Grande Arche de la Défense, a reinterpretation of the Arc de Triomphe located on the Champs-Elysées. Made of concrete, L'Arche included a rooftop restaurant, an exhibition area, and was large enough to fit Notre Dame Cathedral inside of it.

Sharp-dressed pedestrians in business attire hustled across the street and wound their way past enormous outdoor sculptures to enter the hotels, office buildings, restaurants, and stores. A scattering of folks lounged on grass in the green spaces or beneath the shade of one of the blooming cherry blossom trees.

"You doing okay back there?" Hunter glanced at the rearview mirror to get a look at Sable.

"I'm okay," she replied, meeting his eyes in the mirror.

"I'm okay too," Sanchez piped up with amusement.

"I'm not worried about you," Hunter said, returning his attention to the road ahead.

His concern was restricted to Sable. She'd been a bit nervous, but she was the best person for the job. Alissa was doing recon work with Hossam, tracking down a vehicle and other items needed for the weekend.

The sexy siren had disappeared, and Sable didn't look anything like herself. He'd done a heckuva job, if he did say so himself. Her hair was tucked up under a short Afro wig, and a thick mustache covered her upper lip. He'd widened her nostrils with silicone and used brown contacts to hide her hazel eyes. Dental facades changed the shape of her mouth and gave her a different profile.

He'd made some adjustments to the navy-blue suit she wore, but overall it gave her a boxy shape to hide her luscious curves. With a pair of cap-toe Oxfords to complete the look, he was confident no one would be able to tell she was a woman.

Hunter parked the Mercedes sedan and checked the audio and video on the laptop beside him before sliding the computer under the seat. His tie clip obscured a tiny camera. They wanted to bring down the entire operation, and getting

Costas on video accepting a bribe was one of the ways they planned to do it.

He stepped out of the vehicle and opened the back door, and Sanchez exited, wearing a dark suit and fake ponytail attached to the back of his head. Scowling behind aviator sunglasses, he looked dangerous and appropriately suspicious.

Sable slid out of the car with a silver briefcase attached to her wrist by handcuffs. She straightened her shoulders and followed Sanchez.

"Careful with your walk," Hunter murmured under his breath.

Right away, she adjusted to a more masculine stride. When they reached the bank, Hunter opened the door, and they all walked in. A woman with dark hair immediately approached, wearing a smile that looked permanently tattooed on her face.

"*Bonjour. Comment je peux vous aider aujourd'hui?*"

"Do you speak English?" Hunter asked.

"*Oui*, of course. How can I help you?"

"This is Mr. Alfonso Fuentes. We have a meeting with Mr. Costas." Hunter made a subtle movement with his hand, and her eyes lowered to the briefcase strapped to Sable's wrist.

"I understand. Please, come to our private waiting area, and I will make a call upstairs to check Mr. Costas's availability. Right this way." The woman led them to an office with the appearance of a formal sitting room. Heavy wood furniture and rich-colored tapestries adorned the space.

She disappeared but returned in less than one minute. "Mr. Costas will see you now." She gestured toward the elevator with a sweep of her hand. "Take the elevator to the tenth floor, and you will be taken to his office."

"Thank you." Hunter nodded, and they crossed the tile to the two elevators.

Inside, he touched the button for the tenth floor and the doors closed.

"Do you guys ever get nervous doing this?" Sable whispered. She stood in front of him, next to Sanchez.

"All the time," Hunter said.

"I do," Sanchez admitted.

"But...?" she prompted.

"We're good at our job. Pretend you're going to steal something from a bad guy and return it to a good guy," Hunter said.

Sable's narrow shoulders relaxed. "That helped. Thank you."

"Any time."

When they exited the elevator, another woman greeted and guided them down the hall to an office where she knocked lightly on the door.

"Come in," the male occupant called from inside.

The woman opened the door, and they walked in. A middle-aged man with dark hair and black glasses stood behind a desk strewn with papers, folders, and a desktop computer on one end.

"Hello, Mr. Fuentes. I'm Maximo Costas." He extended his hand to Sanchez first.

He took it. "Thank you for meeting with me on such short notice. This is my accountant, John Masekela, and my bodyguard."

"Nice to meet you all. Please, have a seat." Maximo waved a hand toward the leather chairs in front of his desk.

Sable and Sanchez sat down, and Hunter stood behind them.

"Quite a view you have here," Sanchez said.

"One of the perks of working at this bank for a long time and doing a good job," Maximo said with a laugh.

Behind him was the view of one of the small parks in the area, as well as a fifty-foot sculpture known as The Red Spider.

"How can I help you? I understand you're looking for investment opportunities?"

He looked at Sable for a response, but Sanchez drew the banker's attention back to him.

"Correct." Sanchez handed over a business card. "Business is very good at the moment. Sales are exploding in the UK and Spain, and I wish to expand into Eastern Europe. Until then, I want to do some investing here, in France."

"What kind of business are you in?" Maximo asked.

"Pharmaceutical sales."

In the resulting quiet, everyone in the office understood exactly what he meant, and the spark of interest in Maximo's eyes was unmistakable.

"My accountant has advised me it's necessary to save on the dreaded taxes. Opening an account will allow me to move on opportunities as they arise. I've heard good things about your bank—and you in particular."

Maximo's eyebrows raised. "Thank you. I'm flattered."

"The people I know spoke highly of your... discretion."

"Well, of course, we always keep our customers' affairs in the strictest confidence. How much do you have to deposit?"

"One hundred thousand in cash to start, with much, much more to come over the next couple of months."

"How much are we talking about?" the wealth manager asked in a neutral tone.

"Millions."

Costas did his best not to react, but there was no mistaking the indrawn breath.

"I see. Well, for today's deposit, we have paperwork that needs to be filled out, of course. I'm sure you understand, with that amount of money, we have strict regulations to adhere to."

Hunter had expected him to push back at first. Banks were required to fill out suspicious activity reports, also known as SARs.

"Yes, I understand but would prefer if this transaction were handled carefully, as it is of a delicate nature. I'm willing to pay the necessary additional fees to ensure your highest level of confidentiality."

"I'm afraid I can't help you. I'm very sorry." Costas gave a pleasant smile but appeared unmoved.

Sable leaned over and whispered in Sanchez's ear.

Sanchez nodded. "Seems we've come to the wrong place. Excuse me."

They stood.

"Wait a minute!" Costas jumped up from his desk and glanced at Sable. She returned the look without flinching, as Hunter had instructed.

"There are regulations, but I believe we can still accommodate you. I'll need your identification, and the necessary fees will need to be paid today. Have a seat. Please. Let's not be hasty."

Sable glanced at Sanchez and nodded.

"I'm a busy man, Mr. Costas." Sanchez injected the right amount of irritation in his voice.

"I understand."

They reclaimed their seats. "I'd be happy to pay your fee, but..." Sanchez looked pointedly at the camera in the corner and then met Costas's gaze.

The wealth manager slipped his hand below the desk, and the blinking light went out.

Sable then entered the combination on the briefcase and popped the lid. Sanchez removed thick stacks of twenties and dropped them on the desk. "Will this be enough to cover the bank fees?"

Costas snatched up the cash and fanned the edges with his thumb. "Yes, this should cover it. Excuse me while I step out for a few minutes to pull together the necessary paperwork."

He left the office, and Sable let out a soft breath. "He's actually going to do it."

"He's been doing it for years, working with Moreau and probably others. This is nothing for him," Hunter said.

When Costas returned, he was noticeably more upbeat. He'd likely done some digging into the background of Alfonso Fuentes and saw how much he was worth.

"Mr. Fuentes, here is the paperwork I need you to sign, and I will now take your deposit."

He placed the sheets directly in front of Sanchez, and he signed in the appropriate spots.

Costas took them and scanned them, making sure everything was filled out. "Excellent. The cash, please."

Sable handed over the money.

Costas tapped the keyboard and the printer on his desk spewed out a couple of pages, which he then showed to Sable and Sanchez.

"Confirmation of your deposit, as well as your account number." He pulled a business card from his drawer. "This is for you. Each time you need to make a deposit, give me a call, and I'll make sure the entire process goes smoothly. I can also handle any transfers to our Panama branch, where you can be certain of the strictest confidentiality. What kind of assets are you interested in? Stocks, mutual funds?"

"Easy to sell products," Sanchez answered. "I'd also be interested in businesses. If you know of any opportunities, I'd certainly like to be made aware."

"I understand. Trust me, I'll make sure your money is invested in the best financial vehicles."

They all stood and shook hands.

"I'm glad to know I came to the right place after all," Sanchez said.

"Before you go, I might have a lead on an opportunity. I know a businessman who would like to partner with new investors. Do you know much about antique shops?"

"Not much, but if there is money to be made, I'm interested."

"Will you be in the country this weekend?"

"I'll be here until Sunday."

"Excellent. Keep your Saturday night free. I'll see if I can get you an invitation to an elegant affair taking place this weekend, put on by an owner of antique shops. It's the kind of business I'm certain you'd be interested in investing in."

"Do you think you can get me three invitations? My wife and girlfriend are traveling with me, and I don't want to leave them out. They love getting dressed up. You know women."

"I most certainly do." All four of them laughed. Costas' eyes sparkled with interest. "Your wife and your girlfriend, you said?"

"I'm a very lucky man."

"Yes you are. Yes you are indeed." He walked them out to the elevator. "I'm certain I can secure the additional invitations. I'll give you a call later this afternoon to confirm."

Sanchez shook his hand. "Thank you."

The three descended in the elevator to the first floor and quickly returned to the vehicle.

Inside, Sable grunted. "What a scum bag."

Sanchez chuckled, loosening his tie. "How long do you think he'll wait before he calls to confirm, Hunter?"

"Two hours max." Hunter checked the computer and confirmed the conversation in the office had been recorded. The video was sharp, and the sound came through loud and clear. Perfect.

He pulled out of the lot. "I can't wait to nail that bastard and all his friends."

28

B right lights lit up the front lawn, and the trail of luxury vehicles looped around the driveway as guests arrived at Jean-Jacques Moreau's home in the French countryside.

Hunter's hand enveloped Sable's as she stepped out of the silver Rolls Royce. He continued to play the part of bodyguard and driver with the facial hair and wig, and gave her hand a reassuring squeeze as their eyes met. That little contact and a knowing look did plenty for her racing heart.

Returning to the scene of the crime was risky, but a chance she wanted to take to nail the man who ordered her friend's death and framed her for it.

Fortunately, Moreau shouldn't recognize her as the same woman with cornrows who'd broken into his office and escaped with his precious fake Gutenberg Bible. Hunter worked his magic again. This time, she wore brown contacts to hide her distinctive eyes and a short blond wig. The silky strands came down to her chin, with the left side tucked behind her ear and the right covering her right ear.

A gold necklace with a bold medallion hovered above her

cleavage and included an inductive device, which sent audio to the tiny earpiece in her right ear. A one shoulder black sleeveless dress molded to her curves. In a pair of black heels with gold embellishments, she felt sexy and feminine.

Sanchez exited the vehicle next, looking dapper in a black tuxedo. He took Alissa's arm, who exited behind him, regal in a burgundy gown, its loose skirt swirling around her ankles. Diamonds in her ears, and an engagement and wedding ring on her left hand completed the disguise as Sanchez's wife. Overall, the three looked the part of wealth and status and fit in with the other guests.

"Two beautiful women on my arms. What did I do to deserve this?" Sanchez asked as they strolled toward the entrance.

"Stay away from the blond," Hunter warned, his voice loud and clear through the earpiece.

Sanchez chuckled. He liked to tease Hunter, and Sable experienced a jolt of delight each time Hunter expressed jealousy.

Inside, uniformed staff guided them toward the large room where the guests congregated—a sea of evening gowns and tuxedos milled about the room as men and women conversed and politely laughed at each other's jokes.

Almost as soon as they entered, Costas approached. Tonight he wore a white tuxedo, and his face lit up with a grin as broad as a kid's on Christmas morning.

"So glad you could come," he said, practically gushing.

"I wouldn't have missed this for the world. This is my wife, Naomi."

"Nice to meet you." Alissa extended her hand.

"And my... girlfriend, Jessica," Sanchez said with a little laugh.

Sable's stomach tightened with worry. Would Costas recognize her as the same person who came into his office days ago as a male accountant?

"Nice to meet you." He didn't even do a double take. "Let me introduce you to the host, Jean-Jacques Moreau. I told him all about you, Mr. Fuentes. He's anxious to make your acquaintance. Follow me."

As they took off behind him, Sable glanced at Sanchez, and he smiled reassuringly. They passed the first test. If they could fool Moreau, they'd be all set.

Costas led them across the room to where Moreau was talking with a small group of men. As soon as Costas interrupted him, he excused himself and extended a hand to Sanchez. "Great to have you here. Maximo told me all about you and how you want to expand your business in Europe."

"Yes. Currently I'm in the UK and Spain, and he's helping me with my investments here. I'd like to do more on the continent—perhaps in Eastern Europe."

The older man's eyes narrowed with renewed interest. "I'm sure he can help you. He's a good man. Everyone at Banque Quotidienne works hard to ensure their customers are satisfied. That's why I've stayed with them for years. Now, you have to tell me who these lovely ladies are."

Sanchez made the introductions again, and Moreau raised his eyebrows.

"Well, you're very fortunate, Mr. Fuentes." His gaze came back to Sable. "Do I know you?"

She stiffened, her pulse tripping over itself. "No. I—"

"She's done some acting," Sanchez interjected smoothly, rubbing a hand up and down her back. "Small parts here and there. Maybe that's where you know her face from. She filmed a very popular toothpaste commercial—what was it, two years ago, *mi amor*?"

"Yes, that's right." Sable nodded.

"Maybe that's it," Moreau said, nodding slowly. "Of course, I might also be drawn to her lovely face because I have a weakness for blonds."

The three men chuckled while Alissa and Sable smiled politely.

Moreau continued. "My wife used to be an actress, and some Hollywood types are here, so who knows, with a bit of networking you might land a bigger role—if that's something you're interested in."

"I'm definitely interested," Sable said, putting on her brightest smile.

"Let me introduce you to a few people," Moreau offered.

He took them around, and they chatted with politicians, and as he said, a few Hollywood types—a producer and a couple of actors. His wife was friendly, though she seemed to be evaluating the room from her perch on an invisible pedestal.

Before long, Alissa and Sable tuned their earpieces to a different frequency and hovered at the perimeter of the room while Sanchez conversed with Moreau, Costas, and another man Sable didn't recognize. The women surreptitiously surveyed the room, pretending to be in conversation with each other as they fed information through the earpieces.

"Four guards stationed around the room. Not a lot of security, but not light either," Sable said for the benefit of the audio.

Several streets away, Hossam waited in a van with a small team and their tech equipment. Rather than mingle with the other drivers on the property, Hunter remained in the Rolls Royce and also listened.

"I think now is a good time for you to make your move," he said.

Alissa nodded and laughed, as if Sable said something funny. "I agree. We don't have eyes on us, and Sanchez has them preoccupied."

"You should definitely go now," Hossam agreed.

Alissa sauntered over to Sanchez and stroked his arm. "Honey, we're going to run to the little girls' room."

"All right. Don't be long."

"We won't." Alissa gave him a light peck on the cheek.

As they walked away, Sable heard Moreau say, "If only my wife were as open-minded as your wife, I could live a more peaceful existence."

"You have to make sure women understand why it's in their best interest to go along with the plan," Sanchez explained. "Diamonds are a great incentive."

The men laughed, and Sable and Alissa rolled their eyes at each other.

"He's enjoying this way too much," Alissa murmured.

The ladies left the room and walked down a quiet hallway toward the bathroom. Instead of going in, they checked to make sure no one followed them and went past it to a staircase at the back which led to the second floor. The second-floor hallway was empty, so they rushed up the next flight of stairs, which took them to the third floor where Moreau's office was located.

Their gazes swept the area. Finding no one around, they speed-walked to the end of the hall.

"We're here," Alissa said to the men listening.

Sable pulled two tools from between her breasts and stooped in front of the doorknob. She went to work picking the lock while Alissa kept a lookout.

"One second," Hunter said.

Hossam's contacts accessed information at the security company servicing Moreau's home, and they learned the businessman created a partition in his alarm system to isolate the office. No one could break in again while he had guests. From inside the car, Hunter would use a signal jammer to interfere with the Wi-Fi system. The Wi-Fi operated the alarm and hidden camera—which provided a good view of the door.

More than two minutes offline, and the system went into

emergency mode, which meant security would be alerted to start looking for the breach. Because of the last break-in, one of the places they were bound to investigate first was Moreau's office. Moreau would have changed the combination, so Sable needed to crack the safe, swipe the external drive, and she and Alissa had to be out of the office—all in under two minutes.

"Your two minutes start... now!" Hunter said.

With the lock already undone, Sable turned the knob and opened the door, and she and Alissa slipped inside. The room was dark and filled with shadows, so Alissa pulled open the drapes to let exterior light into the room, while Sable removed Moreau's portrait from the wall.

Taking a deep breath, Sable relaxed and concentrated on the task at hand. She placed her ear to the cool surface of the safe and turned the dial, listening for the clicks and grooves in the locking mechanism.

"Fifteen seconds," Alissa said.

Sable swallowed. One number down, two to go. She kept working the dial, moving fast, breathing evenly so she wouldn't lose her concentration.

"Thirty seconds."

Come on baby, she thought. In the past few days she'd gone through plenty of practice sessions on a similar safe at the safe house. She could do this. The last number snapped into place.

"Forty-five seconds."

Sable quickly went through the number variations to find the right combination.

"Sixty seconds."

She heard the sound she needed to hear and turned the lever.

"She got it," Alissa whispered excitedly.

Elated, Sable swung the door open—and her lips fell apart. Her heart plummeted to her heels.

The safe was empty.

29

"It's empty." Sable's head spun in disbelief. This couldn't be happening.

"What did she say?" Hunter and Hossam asked at the same time.

"This can't be right." Sable turned to Alissa.

Alissa shook her head, stunned. "There's nothing in the safe."

"You have less than a minute to get out of there," Hunter said.

"No, we have to stay," Sable implored to Alissa. "We need to find the drive. It has to be here somewhere." She spun in a circle, eyes bouncing around the large room.

"I don't think this is a good idea," Alissa said.

"Ladies, get out of there. Now," Hossam said.

Sable rushed over to Moreau's desk and yanked on the middle drawer. Locked.

"She's not leaving." Alissa cast a worried glance at the door.

"I have to find it. I have to." Frantic, Sable sat on the leather chair and picked the lock.

"You have thirty fucking seconds to get out of there," Hunter growled.

Sable snatched open the drawer and rummaged through the contents. Pens, notes, paper clips. *Where is it!* her mind screamed.

"OK, it's time to go." Lips pressed together in a determined expression, Alissa came around the desk and slammed the drawer shut.

She grabbed Sable by the wrist and pulled her up from the chair. Sable let herself be marched toward the door, disappointment heavy on her shoulders.

The heel of her shoe caught on the edge of the area rug and she tripped, jerking it askew. She glared over her shoulder in annoyance and then did a double take.

Twisting her arm free from Alissa's grip, she pointed at the floor. "Look."

Alissa came to stand beside her. "What is that?"

"A door," Sable said excitedly.

"What is happening?" Hossam asked.

Sable dragged aside the rug and revealed a small door, approximately two feet by two feet, built into the wooden floor. She dropped to her knees and pulled up the handle. Another safe. Of course! Floor safes had become more popular of late.

"There's another safe in the floor," Alissa announced to the men listening.

"You don't have time. You have ten seconds left," Hunter warned.

"This might be where the drive is. You have to let me try to open it," Sable said.

Alissa looked torn.

"Six seconds," Hunter warned. "Five, four—"

"Do you think you can open it?" Alissa asked.

Sable nodded. "It's a Stunson. I've opened one of these

before. I only need three numbers, and I'm certain I can figure out what they are."

"*Zero*. Fuck! Get her out of there!" Hunter yelled.

Sable winced at his voice booming through the earpiece.

"She wants to try," Alissa told him.

"You're going to get caught. Someone from security could show up there any minute. Alissa, get her out of there. *Now*. These people are dangerous."

"She wants to open it, Hunter." Alissa's gaze connected with Sable's. "I'm going to let her."

Thank you, Sable mouthed. She lay on her belly on the floor and put her ear to the safe door.

"Keep the Wi-Fi jammed so security can't see into the office. It'll buy us some time," Alissa said.

They could leave the office and have Hunter jam the Wi-Fi a second time before coming back in, but two interruptions in one night would be suspicious and have the same result. Security would start searching for the breach. Better to power through.

"I'm coming in there," Hunter said.

"No! Let her do her job. If you blow our cover, you'll make the situation worse."

"If anything happens to her..."

"That's why I'm here. I won't let anything happen."

"This might be our only shot, Hunter," Hossam said in a calm but worried voice.

Hunter muttered a stream of curses, and Sable turned off the audio so she could concentrate. Moving forward, she only heard Alissa.

She took big, calming breaths in and out of her mouth and cracked her knuckles. Then she went to work. With quiet all around, she lost herself, concentrating as she spun the dial on the safe. The combination was nothing but a puzzle to be solved, one number at a time.

Alissa gave her room and stood in a corner, watching. Tension vibrated off the other woman, but Sable ignored it and only paid attention to the metal box which contained, she hoped, the proof to set her free.

All of a sudden, the door pushed open, and her head popped up.

"What are you doing?" a large man barked in French. He was huge, at least 6'6 and wide.

He didn't see Alissa behind the door, and Sable knew she needed to keep his attention on her.

"Who are you?" she demanded, as if she had the right to ask questions.

From the corner of her eye, she saw Alissa lift the hem of her dress and slide a knife from a holster between her thighs.

The man marched toward Sable, who scrambled away on her hands and knees. At the sound of a yelp, she turned to see Alissa yanking the knife from the security guard's back. But he didn't fall. Instead, the giant turned around to face his attacker.

Alissa shut the door and kicked off her heels.

Sable watched in amazement as the man stomped toward her, and she deftly slid out of reach, following up with a rolling slice to his arm before spinning quickly away. He roared like an angry bear while she danced around him. Blood dripped from the knife and his arm to the floor, and the man cursed in French, making the wrong decision to rush Alissa with the elegance of an charging bull.

The dance continued, her hand moving fast with diagonal slashes in an "X" motion. Alissa dipped and slid with fleet-footed moves. Each time before she slipped away, she swiped some part of his body with the blade—an arm, a thigh, the center of his chest. But she always stayed out of reach, and Sable understood why. If one of his substantial fists landed, he could shatter the bones in her face.

Sable searched the room for a weapon to help. She clambered to her feet and yanked one of the glass-encased George Washington letters off the wall. It would have to do. She'd smash it over his head.

Hoisting the memento high, she searched for an opening to jump into the fray. Alissa slipped under the man's arm, and without turning to face him, made two quick jabs in his lower back before sliding out of the way.

His movements had already slowed from the multiple cuts and loss of blood. Those last blows were too much for him. Gasping, he staggered and left a red trail as he dragged his hand along the wall, trying not to fall. He fell anyway, dropping to his knees on the blood-dotted floor, his face a mask of agony. Sable froze in position, hands raised with the glass case above her head.

Alissa stabbed the man in the side of the neck, and his eyes rolled back in his head. She kicked him from behind, and he crashed to the floor in his blood soaked suit.

Sable lowered her unused weapon. "Wow. Guess you don't need my help."

Alissa smiled, not even winded. "Did I get any blood on me?" She turned in a full circle.

Sable lifted the folds of the skirt and examined the material. "A couple of dots in the back, but they won't be very noticeable in the folds of the gown. The color of your dress helps."

"All right, you're up. Open the safe so we can get out of here before Mr. Moreau sends a search party after us."

While Alissa wiped her prints off the knife in the man's neck, Sable rushed over to the safe and lay flat on her belly again. A few minutes in, she heard Alissa give an update to Hunter and Hossam.

The men worried about them, but she needed time to complete the task. She'd figured out the three numbers. All she needed to do was try the six possible combinations to see which variation would open the safe.

She tried them all, and the last one worked. She almost cried with relief, tears welling up in her eyes. Uttering a quick prayer that the safe contained what they were looking for, she opened it. Alissa came over to examine the contents.

"She's got it open," she said, for the benefit of Hossam and Hunter.

Sable turned on her earpiece. "I have the drive!" she exclaimed, unable to contain her excitement. Alissa took the device from her hands, and Sable then removed two leather-bound books.

"What are those?" Alissa said.

"What? What else did you find?" Hossam asked.

Sable flipped open one of them. "They're ledgers."

Alissa crouched beside her. "Guys, we need to take these. I can hide the drive in the sling under my dress, but there's no way for us to hide these ledgers and smuggle them out of here."

They looked around the room, searching for an alternative.

Sable's eyes landed on the door leading to the balcony. "I have an idea. We drop the ledgers over the balcony to the grass below, and Hunter can pick them up."

"Good idea."

"I'm on my way to the side of the building now," Hunter said.

Sable opened the door and stepped onto the balcony with the books. She dropped them to the grass below and waited. A minute later, Hunter came around the corner at a brisk walk.

She waved at him, and he shook his head as he gazed up at her.

"I'm beating your ass when you get in the car."

She grinned. "Promises, promises."

Then she went back into office.

Alissa cleaned blood off the bottom of her feet with tissue from Moreau's desk and slipped on her shoes. They wiped everything down, including the doorknobs and the memorabilia case before they exited the room, careful not to step in the blood on the floor.

Both women started down the stairs to the second level.

"You did good back there," Alissa said, admiration in her eyes.

"Thank you."

Alissa stuffed the bloody tissue papers under the trash in the bathroom and then followed Sable to the main room, where Sanchez and the men sat in a corner talking. She sashayed over and sat on her fake husband's lap.

Sable saw the tension on his face because they'd been gone longer than expected.

"I thought you'd gotten lost, *mi amor*," he said, sliding an arm around Alissa's waist. "While you were gone, there was a security breach."

"Oh no," Alissa said.

"Nothing my men can't handle," Moreau said, with a dismissive wave of his hand.

She laughed lightly, back in the character of a doting wife. "Good to hear. Unfortunately, we had a bit of trouble in the bathroom. Jessica threw up. She's not feeling well. I hate to ask you to leave, but..." She gave Sanchez puppy dog eyes.

Sable pressed a hand to her stomach and grimaced. "I'm so sorry, baby."

"Please, don't apologize. If you don't feel well, we must get you home." Sanchez turned to the men. "Gentlemen, we'll have to continue this conversation another time," he said with phony regret. "You know how to reach me, and I know how to reach you. I have a good feeling about you, and I know we'll be doing a lot of business together."

"A lot of business," Moreau said, standing.

Alissa and Sanchez stood. Sanchez slid an arm around his fake wife's waist and took Sable's hand. "Gentlemen, have a good night."

Moreau and Costas looked at him with envy and admiration as the three of them turned away. They didn't speak as they walked out of the large house. Hunter had already pulled the silver Rolls Royce to the front and stood beside it with the door open.

They piled into the backseat, and as soon as they passed through the gates of the estate, Sable let out a squeal of triumph.

"We did it!" She wiped tears of relief from her eyes.

Finally, the nightmare was coming to an end.

Sanchez patted her knee. "Good job."

"Thanks." She leaned forward and caught Alissa's eye. "Thank you. If you hadn't handled the security guard, I wouldn't have been able to finish opening the safe."

Alissa grinned. "It's the least I could do for giving me a break when I don't feel like performing my wifely duties with my very lucky hubby." She captured Sanchez's chin between her fingers and made kissing noises.

"Take your hands off me, woman," he said.

They all had a good laugh.

30

"One more toast!" Sanchez held his shot glass of vodka aloft.

After two days of being on tenterhooks at the safe house while awaiting law enforcement's review of the evidence, Jean-Jacques Moreau was finally going to pay for his crimes. The five of them—Sanchez, Hossam, Hunter, Sable, and Alissa—decided to celebrate. They went out to dinner and afterward ended up in the Latin Quarter, crowded around a small table having drinks in the lively atmosphere of a neighborhood bar.

The former working class neighborhood was renowned for the popular tourist attractions Notre Dame Cathedral and France's prestigious university, La Sorbonne. Because of that, the bar contained a lot of people, many of them students, screaming and guzzling beer and wine with plenty of young tourists among them.

"What are we going to toast this time?" Hossam asked, a glass of Orangina before him.

Sanchez thought for a moment and then said, "How about to making new friends and for justice finally being served?"

"Love it!" Alissa said, glassy-eyed and yelling to be heard above the din.

"Here, here!" they all yelled, tossing back their drinks and then slamming the glasses on the table.

"Listen," Hossam said. He didn't drink alcohol and had consumed only soda the entire night. "I can't thank you all enough. My friends in financial crimes thank you. Really. Moreau has escaped prosecution for years and is finally having to pay for his crimes. All thanks to you."

Hunter flung an arm across Sable's shoulders and pulled her into his side. "It was a team effort. Your people in financial crimes came through, and this little lady got the goods on Moreau."

Sable tilted back her head and gazed up at Hunter. "Like you said, a team effort."

He ached to kiss her but refrained. Later he'd kiss and touch as much as he wanted.

All night he'd been horny and wanting to get her alone. He didn't know if it was the drinking or the high from breaking up one of the largest money laundering operations in Europe, but he found himself constantly touching her, wanting to keep her near.

He caught the look Sanchez and Alissa sent his way and knew they'd drill him for information when he returned to Georgia.

The waitress arrived to inquire if they wanted more drinks or food, but because of the late hour, they all agreed it was time to go. They paid the bill and sauntered out of the bar. Hunter and Sable held hands and pulled up the rear behind the other three as they strolled along.

"Where to now?" Sable asked.

Alissa looped arms with Sanchez. "Me and my husband are going to our hotel because we have an early flight tomorrow."

Hunter didn't miss Hossam's crestfallen appearance.

"I guess this is goodbye," Sable said. "It was nice meeting you, Alissa and Sanchez."

"Likewise," Sanchez said.

The three of them hugged. Then Sable looked at Hossam and gave him a bigger, warmer hug.

"Take care of yourself," he said.

"I will. You too. Until next time."

"Thanks for everything," Hunter said.

After a few more hugs around the group, they disbursed—Sanchez and Alissa going one way, Hossam another, and Sable and Hunter choosing to go for a walk before they returned to Hossam's apartment in Saint-Germain.

As they strolled along the cobblestoned streets holding hands, Sable sighed. "I can't believe the nightmare is really over."

"It is. You don't have to look over your shoulder."

The police had raided Moreau's home and businesses and arrested him and his accomplices. The leather-bound ledgers contained the records of sales at his antique shops going back for years, as well as the amounts laundered through fake invoices and fake expense reports, commissions he earned, and other incriminating evidence. The recordings Hossam and his team captured from the conversation with Sanchez at Moreau's home added additional charges. Law enforcement also discovered incriminating evidence on the external drive, including the full video showing Moreau in the office when his security guard killed Senator Richelieu.

As the police hauled him away in handcuffs, his wife screamed at them with tears flowing down her cheeks. "He hasn't done anything! You monsters won't leave him alone!"

Hunter couldn't deny it was a great performance.

After a brief foot chase, Elan Crimini was in custody but proclaimed his innocence to the cameras. Maximo Costas was arrested, and so were other employees at Banque Quotidienne, including their CEO. The financial crimes unit was busy combing through the bank's records, but a preliminary investigation indicated Crimini and Moreau were the tip of the iceberg. The bank had worked with a number of criminal organizations across Europe for years, helping them launder hundreds of billions of dollars.

Hunter and Sable strolled through the neighborhood hand-in-hand, simply enjoying each other in the silence.

"You know what I just realized?" Hunter asked. "It's my last night in Paris, and I didn't get to go up the Eiffel Tower. I never even visited it."

"You didn't?" Sable sounded shocked.

"No. Too late now. My flight leaves in the morning, so there won't be time to visit unless I go real early, and I'm not *that* interested in seeing it." He laughed. "Next time."

"What time is it?"

Hunter checked his watch. "Fifteen minutes till eleven."

Sable stopped in the middle of the sidewalk. "We still have time."

He stared at her. "Time for what? You want to go there now? I had another idea planned for this evening." He let his voice drop low and placed a hand on her waist.

Sable slipped from his grasp. "We can do that later. We're going to see the tower. They light it up every hour after the sun goes down."

"We don't have to—"

"You have to! The Eiffel Tower is the symbol of Paris, and this is your last chance to see it before you return to Georgia. Next time you visit, you can go up the tower. Trust me, the light show is an amazing experience because there will be tons of people there." She tapped her chin. "The best view is at Trocadéro, but the views from the right bank of the River Seine are nice. Near one of the bridges. Come on, let's go." She grabbed his hand and tugged him along with her.

Hunter laughed. Her excitement was contagious and sparked his own enthusiasm to share the experience with her.

"Taxi!" Sable waved her hand vigorously to catch the attention of a driver. Finally, a man pulled over and they hopped in. Sable told him where to drop them off.

"This better be as good as you say," Hunter warned.

She beamed, her face and eyes bright with a smile. "You won't regret it."

He pulled her close and gave her kiss, pressing his mouth against her warm lips. His fingers climbed into her soft, loose hair, and he looked forward to tugging the soft strands later as they once again made passionate love.

The driver dropped them on the right bank, near Pont Alexandre III with three minutes to spare.

"Pont Alexandre is considered the most beautiful bridge in Paris because of the gilded structures and designs," Sable explained.

She rested her forearms on the stone wall and looked down at the water. Small groups of people loitered on both sides of the river, waiting for the light show.

Hunter came behind Sable and caged her in, his gaze sweeping their surroundings. The majestic Eiffel Tower reached skyward, encased in a golden glow across the River Seine on the left bank. The dark water reflected the lights from the surrounding buildings and open-air boats cruising downstream.

He brushed his nose along the side of Sable's neck and inhaled the sweet floral scent of her skin.

"What are your plans when you get back to Tennessee?" he asked.

She leaned back against him. "Well, my daughter—" She broke off when an audible grasp went up from the people around them.

The show had begun. Lights danced the full length of the

tower, twinkling off and on in a choreographed display that captured the attention of everyone nearby. The spectacle went on for five full minutes, and Hunter took several photos but mostly just enjoyed the eye-catching performance on one of the world's most iconic landmarks.

When the show finished, Sable turned to face him with a big grin on her face. "Well? Was it worth it?"

"You're acting like you put on the show."

"Did you like it or not?" she demanded.

Hunter chuckled. "Yes. Damn." He kissed her cheek and lowered his voice. "I liked it a lot. Thanks. Now I can go back to Georgia and confirm that I saw the Eiffel Tower."

"Exactly."

He wrapped his arms around her and indulged in another kiss. This time, mouth to mouth. Then hand-in-hand, they walked alongside the water to the bridge and started across to the left bank.

As they passed a group of women, one of them turned and said, "Hunter?"

He paused, surprised when he recognized the tall brunette. "Brigitte."

Gaze dipping to where Hunter and Sable held hands, she raised her eyebrows. "I see why you not call to me," she said with a thick accent.

"Yeah. I..." Caught off guard, Hunter didn't have a good explanation. The truth was, he'd simply been looking for a good time with Brigitte, and Sable had erased thoughts of her and all other women from his mind.

"I understand," she said, with more sadness than he'd expected. "*Au revoir*." She waved.

"*Au revoir*."

He and Sable continued on their way.

"Who was that?" she asked, eyes straight ahead.

"No one. Just a woman I met at a club."

"One of your hookups?" she asked lightly, glancing at him.

"Yes, but it was nothing."

"Hey, I'm not judging. This is Paris, after all."

She shrugged, and he couldn't tell if she was affecting a nonchalant attitude or really didn't care.

Near the base of the Eiffel Tower, a man sold crepes, and Hunter ordered a hazelnut one for himself. After some protests about the lateness of the hour, Sable admitted she wanted one too, and he bought one filled with strawberry jam for her.

They decided not to catch another taxi and continued their leisurely stroll back to the apartment, eating their crepes, laughing and talking.

By the time they arrived at the apartment, Hunter's body was humming with desire. He wasted no time stripping Sable of her clothing and then tossing his aside.

With the curtains open to the night, her cries of ecstasy bounced off the white walls as they made love on the cool sheets on their last night in Paris.

31

Sable stretched in bed as sunlight poured through the windows.

Today was a good day. She was going home.

She slipped from the bed and pulled on Hunter's discarded T-shirt lying on the floor. Where was he?

Last night, strolling the streets of Paris before coming back to Hossam's apartment to make love was the perfect way to end the trip.

She found Hunter cooking in the kitchen, fully dressed in jeans and a purple T-shirt draped over his fine physique in such a way, she immediately wanted to jump his bones.

"Hey, good morning," she said, resting her head against the door jamb.

He turned away from the stove for a second, his appreciative gaze sweeping her body down to her toes. "Good morning. I was going to bring you breakfast in bed for our last day."

"Oh no, I spoiled the surprise."

He laughed, gray eyes sparkling with amusement. "It's all good. Now get your pretty ass back into bed and pretend I didn't tell you."

Sable grinned, preening under the compliment. "I think I'll do that."

She scampered away. In the bathroom, she washed up and then returned to the bedroom and tucked her own surprise for him under a pillow.

Hunter came in with a tray of food—plump, delicious-looking strawberries, French toast, and scrambled eggs. "For you, my dear."

Sable did a little dance and accepted the tray. "Mmm, this looks delicious. Are you eating?"

"Yes, but I wanted to bring your food first. Now I'll get mine."

"I'll wait until you get back before I start."

He returned with a tray of the same meal, only larger portions. He joined her on the bed, and they both sat back against the pillows and enjoyed the food.

"This is so good," Sable said.

After they finished eating, she set aside the tray and smiled at Hunter.

"Why do you have that look on your face?" he asked, eyes narrowed.

"Because *I* have a surprise for *you*."

"I don't like surprises."

"Well, you're going to have to accept this one."

"What is it?"

"Stop looking so suspicious! I'm not going to stab you. Sheesh." Sable pulled the gift from under the pillow—a rectangular package wrapped in plain brown paper and tied with twine. She folded her feet under her butt and presented it with both hands. "This is for you."

Hunter stared for a moment, as if afraid to touch it. She suspected he knew what was under the paper.

"Take it," she insisted, anxious to see his expression.

He took the gift and slowly removed the twine. Then he

peeled off the paper and revealed a worn copy of *Les fleurs d'amour* by Amelie Sasson, his mother. Sable covered the cost of the rare find because she'd wanted to gift him the novel.

"You found it," he whispered.

"Not me. The *bouquiniste*, Robert, did. There's an inscription inside." She was most excited about this part—more than the actual book. She opened the cover and revealed the dedication written in French.

Pour mon fils. Tu me manques. Je t'aime, toujours. Maman.

"What does it say?" he asked in a thick voice. He hadn't taken his eyes from the book since he tore off the wrapping.

Sable translated. "To my son. I miss you. I love you, always. Mommy." Her throat tightened with tears all over again, like the first time she read the words.

"To my son." Emotion thickened his voice.

"She didn't forget you, Hunter. You might never know why she left you with your father, and why she didn't come after his passing, but she loved you. And she didn't forget you."

"She didn't forget me." He let out a shaky laugh and looked at her with wet eyes. "Thank you. I needed this."

He leaned over and gave her a kiss.

"All right, enough of that." Hunter cleared his throat and rolled off the bed. He picked up his tray. "We need to talk about our plans for when we get back to the States."

"What do you mean?" Sable was genuinely confused. "I have to pick up my daughter from college."

"I'm talking about us. You and me."

"You and me?"

He lowered the tray to the bed. "Yes."

"I mean, I guess we could stay in touch."

"You guess?"

Sable hadn't expected this conversation. She'd assumed their relationship was simply a fling. They'd say goodbye and go their separate ways. Her feelings for Hunter, no matter how intense, would be swept under the rug once she returned state-side. As far as she was concerned, they didn't have a future together, but he seemed to be hinting otherwise.

"I don't know what your expectations are, but we live in different states," she pointed out.

"Hopevale, Georgia isn't far from Nashville, Tennessee."

"Hunter, you're not seriously thinking we're going to be together after we leave here, are you?"

"I was until just now. What is the problem with us contin-uing to see each other?"

Sable climbed off the bed and faced him across the mattress. "You're suggesting we keep in touch long distance, but let's be honest, you're not the settling-down type. We estab-lished your penchant for sleeping around from the beginning."

"I don't need you to tell me what type of person I am."

"You admitted yourself you're a player, and we had fun, but I have no expectations of anything else from you." The last thing she wanted was to get blindsided the way poor Brigitte had been last night.

A bitter laugh left his mouth, and he paced away from her, running a hand over his head. When he faced her again, his eyes were a stormy gray, and a frown of anger marred his fore-head. "What are you saying?"

"It's... my life is crazy. I don't have space for anyone else. I'm still trying to figure things out. My big payday never happened, and I'm a witness in the trial against Jean-Jacques Moreau, which means I'll have to come back here to testify at some point."

"I'm also a witness. I have to testify we fought for our lives in the basement of the cafe. I have to testify the reason I injured two police officers is because they were going to kill us."

Her agitation kicked up a notch. "It's not just the case—there's Avril. I need to make sure she's okay. She's my everything, and I can't let anything or anyone jeopardize my relationship with her."

He studied her in silence, and she wondered what he was thinking.

"How would I jeopardize your relationship with your daughter?"

She didn't have an answer. She'd thrown out the first excuse that entered her head. "It would be hard to balance everything with you and making plans for a business I have to figure out how to finance because the Bible turned out to be fake. We... we wouldn't work. I'm sorry."

And she couldn't risk it. She couldn't risk making any more mistakes where men were concerned. She'd made enough to last a lifetime. Paris with him—the moments when they weren't running for their lives—was fun, with memories she'd treasure forever.

But she wanted permanence. Stability. Hunter would only complicate her life and mess with her head, keeping her from attaining the goals she aimed for.

He laughed dryly. "I see. And *I'm* the player?"

"I wasn't playing a game." She folded her arms across her abdomen. She couldn't look at him. Despite knowing this decision was coming, it was still hard as hell.

"Going home to your friend with benefits now?" His acerbic tone dripped with sarcasm and practically burned a hole in her conscience.

"What I do in Tennessee isn't your concern."

"It is my concern! I care about you, Sable. I think that—"

She flinched. *I love you.* That's what he'd been about to say. She could hear the words as clear as day, though he didn't utter them.

She wanted him to complete the sentence yet didn't want him to complete the sentence. If he said the most intense, beautiful, soul-searing words in the world, she might not be able to walk away.

He didn't.

"Thanks for letting me know," Hunter said in a frosty voice. He left the room with his tray.

For the next hour, awkward silence filled the apartment. Their flights departed forty-five minutes apart, but they had planned to ride to the airport in one car and sit at her gate together. She wanted those last moments with him before she boarded her flight, before he went to *his* gate, and got on *his* flight. Those last moments together wouldn't happen now.

The car to take them to the airport arrived on time, and they took their luggage downstairs.

"*Bonjour!*" the driver said to them both.

"*Bonjour,*" they both returned with much less cheer.

The man loaded Sable's suitcase in the car, and she climbed into the vehicle, scooting over so Hunter could join her. Instead, he closed the door.

Shocked, she rolled down the window. "What are you doing?"

They'd both changed into nicer clothes for travel. He wore a pale-yellow shirt with the sleeves rolled almost to his elbows and the top buttons undone, revealing his strong throat and a glimpse of the blond hairs on his chest. His charcoal slacks were tailored to show off his narrow hips and powerful thighs, and the finishing touch were the black Italian leather shoes on his feet. He looked like he was on his way to a photo shoot rather than a flight home.

"My ride is coming," Hunter said with a nod. Another car pulled in behind them.

"Hunter, you're overreacting." Surely he wouldn't send her away in such a cold, brusque manner?

His face turned into a stony mask. "No, I'm reacting the right way. I want to see you in the States, but you're not interested. I don't think we should waste each other's time. We can take separate cars to the airport."

Her hand gripped the handle inside the car. "So, I'm wrong for being honest with you?"

"No, you were right to be honest with me. You gave me the option to make an informed decision, which I appreciate. Goodbye, Sable. I wish you the best."

He walked toward the other vehicle, and the driver hopped out and took his bags.

"Ready, *mademoiselle*?" Her driver had climbed into the car and slid behind the wheel, but she hadn't noticed.

"Yes." Sable blinked back tears. "I'm ready."

He pulled away from the curb.

32

H unter slammed his fists into the punching bag at The Cordoba Agency gym.

Left. Right. *Jab, jab, jab.*

He circled the bag in a light-footed dance, sweat trickling down the sides of his face. He didn't wear gloves, only hand wraps as he practiced his punches. For years he had practiced this way, or bare-knuckled, several times a month. The conditioning toughened his knuckles and strengthened his wrists and forearms, allowing him to land powerful punches and cause serious damage to his opponents.

If only he could toughen the organ in his chest so he couldn't feel anymore.

The last time he saw Sable replayed over and over in his head. Her hair in large, bouncy curls touching her shoulders and low-heeled sandals showing off her small feet and red-painted toenails. An orange sleeveless dress popped against her nutmeg-brown skin and left little to the imagination, clinging to her fit body in all the right places and highlighting her curvaceous hips and full breasts.

As if that wasn't enough, the scorching memory of the few

times they made love haunted his nights and days. He couldn't forget her sweet voice and the way her gasps ended on a whimper right before she came. Those noises were no longer his. They belonged to someone else now, and he punched the bag harder at the thought of her screwing some nameless, faceless chump.

Since his return to the United States, he'd been discombobulated. He was used to being in control, but she'd knocked him off-balance and refused to give up residence in his head. He couldn't understand how someone he'd only known for a short time could become so important to him.

Her missed everything about her. Her badass hard-headedness. Her kindness to him, her courage in the face of adversity, her strength as a single mother—raising a child on her own into an intelligent, capable adult.

Damn, he missed her. Her laugh was an elixir that could chase away sadness and discomfort. He'd wanted to bottle the sound, but not for mass consumption, too greedy and selfish to share. He'd wanted to be the only one to uncork the bottle and experience every peal of laughter all by himself.

Right. Left. *Punch, punch, punch.*

His muscles burned with the effort of pushing his body past its limit. But he couldn't stop. This pain was easier to bear than the pain of her rejection.

"How much longer are you going to beat the crap out of the punching bag?" Alissa came into view wearing shorts and a tank top, hands settled on her hips. Her natural hair was no longer straightened, styled today in a single Afro puff atop her head.

He barely looked at her.

Left. Right. *Punch, punch, punch.*

"For as long as it takes."

"Why are you punishing yourself?" she asked.

"I'm not."

"Obviously, you are. You've been pushing your body to one hundred and fifty percent since we've been back. Do you want to talk about it?"

"No."

Right. Left. *Strike, strike, strike.*

Hunter moved around the bag so he wouldn't have to see Alissa.

She was persistent, however, and sauntered into his line of sight. Her lips pursed in a disapproving flat line, as if she were his mother.

"I know this is about Sable."

At the mention of her name, Hunter clenched his teeth and hit the bag harder. *Punch. Punch. Punch.*

Alissa walked over and held the bag steady. "Call her."

He stopped punching, chest heaving as he glared at his friend. "Don't you have anything better to do?"

"Besides rescue you? No, I don't." She tossed a fake smile at him.

"I don't need your help, or psychoanalysis, or whatever it is you think you're doing."

"What I'm doing, is giving you advice as a friend, and also as a woman."

"What's going on over here?" Sanchez ambled over and tossed a towel to Hunter.

Hunter mopped the sweat off his face and neck.

"Talk to your boy. He won't listen to me, so maybe he'll listen to you," Alissa said.

"Is it about what you and I were talking about?" Sanchez asked.

She nodded.

"The two of you been talking about me? Wonderful," Hunter said sarcastically. He picked up his Gatorade from the floor and squirted green liquid into his mouth.

"It's only because we're worried about you, *amigo*. We saw

how you behaved with Sable in Paris, and let's be honest, you've never been that way with any other woman before."

"You really seemed to like her. What happened?" Alissa asked.

"I told you what happened. She thinks I'm a player and doesn't want to have anything to do with me."

"Do you like this woman?"

He let his head fall back and stared up at the ceiling in exasperation. "I already told you. I like her, but I'm not chasing after anybody."

Like her was an understatement. Almost from the beginning he'd known he was in trouble. His attraction to Sable had been immediate and deep—deeper than sexual. Sure, she was beautiful and had a great body, but they had a connection, one that made him feel possessive. Protective. He wanted to slay dragons and lay their carcasses at her feet.

She seldom left his thoughts and made him think about things he'd never seriously contemplated before—marriage, starting a family. He'd never been one to limit himself to one woman, and any country or city he spent time in, he always found a way to hook up. Because of her, he completely forgot about Brigitte. No doubt about it, Sable made him want to leave every other woman behind and... settle down.

"Oh, so you're going to let pride get in the way. Am I hearing you correctly?" Alissa asked.

"No, Alissa. I'm going to use common sense and recognize the woman I was involved with doesn't feel the same way about me that I do about her."

Sanchez sucked his teeth. "I think you're making a mistake. In Paris, the two of you were basically a couple. Did you ever consider she might be scared, and that's why she pushed back against the two of you continuing your relationship here in the States?"

"I have, but she has a mouth. She can talk. Sable is not a shy woman or a woman who let's fear keep her from acting. You saw that yourself."

"Can I tell you a secret, as a woman?" Alissa asked.

Hunter debated whether he wanted more advice. He allowed Alissa one more chance to speak her mind. "What do you have to say?"

"She's waiting on your call."

He let out a hearty laugh. "That's it? That's your revelation?"

"Yes, and frankly it's quite good. Here's the deal. Women want to be chased just as much as men enjoy chasing."

Hunter mulled her words but ultimately shook his head in disagreement. He was not putting himself out there to be embarrassed. Besides, Sable didn't want to stay in touch anyway, and plenty of other women would jump at the chance to be with him. Granted, he hadn't connected with any of them since his return, but he planned to—as soon as he got his mind right. Getting his mind right meant purging Sable Devereaux from his thoughts.

Somehow.

"Thank you for such groundbreaking information. I will use it with any future women I date. Anything else?"

"Why are you determined to make yourself suffer?" Sanchez asked. "You have a woman right here telling you what it takes to win your woman back."

"And I thanked her. Now if the two of you will excuse me, I'm going to buy lunch. I'm starving."

"You're always starving," Alissa said.

He shot her two middle fingers, and she shot them right back.

He peeled the wraps off his hands and picked up the Gatorade bottle. Then he walked away.

"Hunter!" Alissa called.

He kept walking and didn't respond. He wanted to be left alone. He didn't need anyone to tell him what to do to win

Sable. The problem wasn't winning her. The problem was she didn't want to be won. All that bullshit about *Hunter, talk to me.* Well, he'd bared his soul and look what happened. Didn't matter to her.

He had his pride.

Hunter Miller didn't push up on anyone who didn't want him.

33

"Mom, you overdid it," Avril signed.

Sable placed the last plastic bag in the trunk of the car. "I can never overdo it where you're concerned. Take the cart for me, please. What do you want for dinner? I was thinking Thai. Chicken or beef?"

"I want you to stop worrying."

"Not one of the choices. Do you want—"

Avril turned her back and pushed the cart toward the corral.

"That's rude!" Sable yelled, though her daughter couldn't hear her.

When Avril was little, if Sable fussed at her, she'd close her eyes so she couldn't see her signing. Turning her back was the teenaged version of the same behavior.

She'd been back in the States for two weeks. After returning to Tennessee, she went to DC to pick up Avril from her dorm now the semester was over.

In another week, Avril would be leaving for her summer job at Microsoft, and Sable wanted to make sure her daughter had everything she needed. Yesterday they'd shopped for new clothes, and today she'd spent over one hundred dollars at Walmart buying additional items.

Maybe she had overdone it, but she was so proud of Avril and wanted her to have a great experience. Her work at Microsoft would benefit other hearing-impaired people, but Sable's stomach tangled in knots at the thought of her daughter being on her own in a completely different state. This was worse than when she dropped her off at college months ago. Then, she'd driven to a gas station and cried for thirty minutes, debating if she had made the right decision.

Did all parents experience the same conflicting emotions? The need to protect your offspring while at the same time trying to give them enough freedom to be independent? The delicate balancing act created the worst feelings of confusion and dread.

She waited until Avril climbed in the car. "That was rude," she signed.

"I know. I'm sorry."

"I worry about you."

"You don't have to worry all the time."

Sable's hands moved more rapidly. "Of course I do! You're my daughter. You're my everything."

Avril didn't respond at first. When she did, there was compassion in her eyes. "I shouldn't be."

Sable turned away and started the car.

Avril tapped her on the shoulder, forcing Sable to face her. "You need to have your own life. I shouldn't be your everything. Let me grow up. I'll be fine, and when I need you, I know I can call you."

Sable smiled, saddened by the words yet proud her daughter expressed her views in a concise, articulate way. "Who is the adult and who is the child?"

Avril laughed. "I love you, Mom."

"I love you too, honey. Be patient with me, okay? It's not easy letting go."

Avril's grin broadened. "Okay."

Sable patted her thigh and pulled out of the parking lot. On the way home, they picked up food from a Thai restaurant nearby.

When her daughter turned fourteen, she purchased the house they currently lived in. It wasn't large by any means, but it provided stability—something she didn't have growing up. The little yellow house with green shutters sat on a street alongside other homes the same size, with carports instead of garages.

She pulled into the driveway and popped the trunk. Avril took the food and removed some of the bags, and Sable loaded her hands with the rest of them. She followed behind her daughter, but they both came to a standstill when they saw the man sitting on the front steps.

Hunter.

More than once she'd picked up the phone to call him. More than once her daughter had asked if she were okay when she caught Sable staring off into space. Each time she shook off the melancholy and reminded herself she didn't need anyone and did fine on her own. Now the reason for her erratic behavior and moments of sadness sat in front of her.

Avril turned to look at her mother, eyes questioning if she knew him. Sable answered the silent question with a nod.

Hunter came to his feet. "Hi. Sorry to intrude."

"How did you find me?"

"It wasn't hard," he replied.

Of course not for someone like him.

"I considered calling first, but I thought it would be better to just come see you, and on the drive up, I figured out what I wanted to say. Do you have a few minutes to talk?"

"Sure," Sable replied, still in a daze. "Let me take these bags inside."

"Okay." His eyes drifted to Avril and then back to her.

Sable and Avril took the bags inside the house to her daughter's bedroom.

"Who is the man outside?" Avril signed.

"A friend. We met on my last trip to Paris."

Avril wiggled her eyebrows. "He's cute."

"He's a friend."

"Sure."

Sable pursed her lips, and Avril fell on the bed, laughing.

"Put away your things. I'll go see what he wants." She took a quick look in the floor-length mirror on the outside of Avril's closet door.

Hunter looked scrumptious in a polo shirt and fitted jeans. Thank goodness she had taken care with her own appearance —hair cascading in loose waves around her face and makeup on point. Skinny jeans showed off her figure, and the tight blue tank exposed her toned arms.

Should she touch up her makeup, or would that be obvious?

"Go!" Avril signed.

"Don't rush me!" Sable signed back.

Taking a deep breath, she exited the room. Out on the porch, Hunter watched the neighbor watering his lawn across the street.

"Hi," Sable said.

"Hi."

He looked so good her heart ached. She wanted to fling herself in his arms. Her daughter kept her busy, but not busy enough to avoid missing his kisses and holding him. She missed his sexy body, laughing gray eyes, and the way he held her in comforting hugs that conveyed she could count on him.

"What brought you all the way to Tennessee?"

"Couldn't stop thinking about you." He spoke in a matter-of-fact voice.

"Oh," Sable said softly.

"I thought about what you said, about me not being the settling-down type, and you're right. I was that guy at one time. Before I met a sexy, trilingual thief who messed up my vacation. The few days I'd taken off, the first in a long time, I ended up almost getting killed and eventually helped bust up a multinational money laundering operation."

Sable bit the inside of her cheek to keep from laughing.

"I messed up back in Paris, Sable. I let my pride get in the way when you told me your thoughts. Thoughts you had every right to express because I'd given you the impression I wasn't the kind of man who could be serious. I'm thirty-three years old, and I've never been in love. Until I met you."

Her heart cracked open. "Hunter…"

"Hear me out. This isn't a line. I *mean* it. I want a future with you, and I'm willing to do what it takes to make that happen. I don't have a family, except the people I work with, and I want to create a family with you. I want someone to come home to, I want babies, I want to cook dinner together and learn history and French and everything about you."

Her mouth fell open. "I-I don't know what to say."

"Say you'll give me a shot," he said, eyes intense. "Let me prove I'm the kind of man you can do long-term with. Not a player, but husband material. And as soon as you're okay with it, I want you to introduce me to your daughter."

Sable suddenly became uncomfortable in her own skin and wrapped her arms around herself. "Meeting my daughter is a big step. I've never introduced a man to Avril. She's been through enough."

"Because of her father," he guessed.

Sable nodded. "I told you that eventually I stopped trying to establish paternity, but I never badmouthed him to her. He was only a year older than me when she was born and under his parents' influence, but he's at the age now where he can fix their relationship, yet he hasn't. That's the hardest part, you know? She has younger siblings, but he won't acknowledge her. It's not about the money, which rightfully he should have helped me take care of her. I struggled for a long time. I would forgive all of that if he would acknowledge her, but he and his parents have always pretended she doesn't exist. Their loss. She's a great kid—hard-headed sometimes, but loving and sweet and kind. Smart. I hit the jackpot with her. I wish I could fix their relationship because I know it hurts, and sometimes I feel so guilty. I could have chosen better."

Hunter frowned, his expression fierce. "You can't blame yourself for his behavior. I still can't believe they've never helped you with her."

"Not once. Not even to buy a pack of diapers. We were on our own. We've always been on our own." She sighed. "One night we were talking in Paris, and you said parents' actions can hurt their kids, and you were right. I feel awful because of what my decisions have put her through. I still don't know how she ended up being such a well-adjusted kid, but she is."

"A testament to you," Hunter said.

Sable gave him a wan smile, and silence settled between them.

Finally, his chest heaved as he took a deep breath. "I should go."

"You drove four hours only to stay a few minutes and then turn around and leave?"

"Well, you haven't responded to what I said earlier, and I don't want to pressure you."

"Then here's my answer. You know what you said before—about you and me having a future together? I want to try. And... since you're here. I would love to introduce you to my daughter now."

He raised his eyebrows. "You're sure?"

"Yes. I'm sure. Believe me, she's already a fan. She thinks you're cute."

He let out a hearty laugh. "Wait, I need to show you something." He signed hello and spelled out his name.

Sable's mouth fell open. "You've been practicing!"

"I didn't know what would happen today, but I wanted to be prepared, just in case. So, that was good?"

"So good. You'll be bilingual in no time."

"You got jokes."

She giggled at his annoyed expression. "You *will*. It just takes time and practice."

She preceded him to the door, but Hunter caught her hand and pulled her around to face him. He hauled her onto her toes in a warm hug and buried his face in her neck.

"Missed you," he whispered.

Her heart filled to the brim with happiness. She smoothed her arms up his biceps, caressed his broad shoulders, and then folded her arms around his neck. Inhaling a deep breath, she reveled in the scent of cucumber-mint on his skin.

They'd only known each other for a short period, but the length of time didn't matter. In less than two weeks, she'd lived a lifetime with Hunter. Now her guard was down, she could fully trust him and experience the kind of relationship she'd always dreamed of.

"Missed you too, Hunter."

He kissed her, his soft lips applying gentle pressure against her mouth. She leaned into him and tightened her arms around his neck.

When they separated, she smiled, and the butterflies that used to fill her belly in Paris returned. Hunter was here, and by the look in his eyes, she'd never have to be alone again.

"How do you feel about Thai food?" she asked as she opened the door.

"Love it."

In the living room, her daughter watched TV with the captions on. When Sable came in, she stood.

"This is my friend, Hunter Miller. He's staying for dinner," she signed.

Hunter did the sign for "Hello," and her daughter's face broke out in a grin.

She returned the greeting.

"Nice to meet you," Hunter signed.

"Nice to meet you too."

Watching them together, joy Sable never experienced before filled her chest.

Thank goodness Hunter came to find her.

34

"G o, *mijo!*" Cruz yelled.

"Go, Alex, go!"

Saturday morning at the soccer field, and members of The Cordoba Agency screamed at the top of their lungs as if they were watching the FIFA World Cup. Cruz's four-year-old son, Alex, led the pack of kids, running and kicking the ball toward the goal with shocking agility for a child his age.

Cruz's wife, Shanice, had stayed home with their new baby girl, but the closest members of the staff had shown up. Raheem—a whiz with computers and The Cordoba Agency's vice president of technology—and his fiancée, Katherine, hollered and clapped at the top of the stands. Sable and Hunter stood below them with Kinsey, whom everyone called Mouse. She was the youngest member of the team—petite and a sniper. Sanchez and Alissa were below them, yelling and waving as if their erratic movements would help the toddler perform better. Meanwhile, Cruz jogged along the sidelines yelling encouragement to his son.

When little Alex kicked the ball into the net and scored, the spectators went wild. It was the end of the game, and he scored the only goal.

Alex turned to his father for approval. His little face broke into a big grin, and he ran off the field toward him. Cruz hoisted his son in the air as the crowd continued to whoop and holler. A proud papa if there ever was one.

Once the celebrating died down, the kids went over to the snack table, and Cruz walked over to where the members of his team remained seated in the stands.

He rubbed his hands together. "All of you are invited to the house in a couple of hours to celebrate. We'll have lunch."

"Did you get Shanice's permission before you invited us?" Katherine teased.

His face broke out in a smile. "Of course. She'll be happy for the company, trust me. You know how Shanice is."

True enough, Shanice was a social person, and the team members often went to their house for Sunday dinner. They only stopped because of her difficult pregnancy.

"I'm in! I'm not passing up free food, and I want to see the baby," Alissa said.

"Good. Then I'll see you all later. Be there at twelve," Cruz said, backing away.

Hunter and Sable climbed down the stands and followed the others to the parking lot.

Hunter flung an arm across Sable's shoulders. "Where are you headed?" he asked Kinsey.

"Home to feed my cat. I might do some target practice before I go over to Cruz and Shanice's. Where you guys headed?"

"I have an errand to run. We'll be over later," Hunter said. "Bye, everybody!"

They all waved as they went to their separate vehicles.

"What errand do you have to run?" Sable asked, snapping in her seatbelt.

They'd spent the last month working on their relationship. Although Hunter initially said Nashville and Hopevale were not that far apart, the distance aggravated him. On Sunday, Sable would be driving back to Tennessee for work on Monday. He wanted to be with her all the time, and she felt the same way. He wanted to fix their predicament today and hoped she wouldn't think they were moving too fast.

"I have something to show you. Well, a couple of things to show you."

They drove into downtown Hopevale. With a flourishing art and music scene and a downtown experiencing fast growth, the little city approximately thirty-five minutes east of Atlanta was turning into a popular destination for people who wanted small-town living with all the amenities of a big city. Because of the warm summer weather, plenty of people strolled through the main street, visiting the retail stores and other businesses.

He pulled in front of an empty storefront with a brick facade and a *FOR LEASE* sign in the window.

"What's this?" Sable asked, unsnapping her belt.

"Part one of what I need to show you. Come on."

Hunter opened the door to the store, and they stepped inside the dusty interior of unused retail space.

"What do you think?"

She placed her hands on her hips, a frown marring her forehead. "Roomy, lots of place, great location for a store."

"It's yours if you want it. For your antique shop. I talked to the landlord, and they don't have any other offers at the moment. If you like it, I'll cover the lease for a year."

Her eyes widened. "Wh-what? No. Hunter, I don't live here."

"Not now, but I want you to. This space is five thousand square feet—not as much as the place you wanted in Nashville, but maybe you can make it work? And take a look out the window. You can see Shanice's bookstore up the street, so you'll have a friend in the neighborhood."

Sable peered out the window, and he waited with a knotted stomach in the silence.

"Good foot traffic," she remarked.

She turned to face him again, but he couldn't read her expression. Was she happy or underwhelmed?

"Oh, and there's this." He pulled a folded envelope from his back pocket and handed it to her.

"Another surprise?" Sable opened the envelope and gasped at the contents. "Hunter, what is this?"

"A gift for your daughter, so you'll never have to worry about her well-being again. By the time she retires, she'll be a multimillionaire."

A brokerage account in Avril's name included fifty thousand dollars in a high yield money market account and over one million in an index fund.

She shook her head and thrust the paper at him. "No. I can't accept this. Leasing a building is one thing, but I can't accept this much money from you."

"It's not my money," he said in a calm voice. "The money came from her father."

Her hand dropped to her side. "How? There is *no* way Andrew willingly gave up money to take care of Avril."

"You're right, he didn't do it willingly. He probably doesn't know the funds are gone. I asked Raheem for a favor, and he pulled that off with his computer voodoo. He's kind of good at taking from the bad guys too. Consider that money back child support." Her mouth fell open, and Hunter stepped closer and took her hand. He rubbed a thumb over her delicate skin. "I'm not doing this because I'm a nice guy. I'm selfish as hell and have an ulterior motive. I want you to move here so we can be together all the time. Sell your house in Tennessee, or rent it out as a safety net, in case things don't work out between us, but I want you here, Sable. I want us to find a place and move in together."

He wanted them under the same roof, and he wanted the honor—the privilege—of taking care of her and providing whatever she needed.

She blinked in shock, but then a smile broke out on her lovely face. "You're serious."

He dropped his voice. "I'm tired of sleeping alone. I need you beside me. Every time I have to leave Nashville or you have to leave here, a piece of my soul is ripped out."

Her lower lip trembled. "I feel the same way. Every single time I have to say goodbye."

"So why keep torturing ourselves? Let's be together. Move to Hopevale."

She laughed and bit her bottom lip. "How can I refuse? This is the perfect spot for an antique shop. I just have to get inventory. My daughter is set for life, and I have you—a wonderful man in my life. I used to think stealing the fake Gutenberg Bible was the worst mistake I'd ever made, but maybe not. A lot of bad things happened for sure." She let out a dry laugh. "But I also met you. So maybe it wasn't such a bad decision. Maybe it was the best decision I ever made."

"So your answer is yes?" Hunter prodded, taking her waist in his hands and pulling her against him. He was already excited about making love to her each night and rolling over in the morning to pull her soft body close.

"My answer is absolutely yes!" she screamed.

Hunter released a whoop of joy and grabbed her up in his arms, spinning them in a circle. Sable flung her arms around his neck and her legs around his waist.

"Hunter, you're so good to me. You're everything I was

looking for. I mean that." She whispered the words while looking deeply into his eyes.

"We both got lucky," he said. "Love you, babe."

"Love you."

When he kissed her, he felt as if his life was starting anew.

And it was.

ALSO BY DELANEY DIAMOND

More books in The Cordoba Agency series!

Until Now (The Cordoba Agency #1)

For Cruz Cordoba, a simple off-the-books assignment becomes a race of life and death.

Until Death (The Cordoba Agency #2)

The best laid plans can still go awry . . . in the most terrifying way. Read the exciting conclusion to Cruz and Shanice's love story.

Heart Stealer (The Cordoba Agency #3)

Katherine was older, sophisticated, and years ago she broke Raheem's heart. Now he must keep her alive and his desire in check. Easier said than done.

Audiobook samples, free short stories, and my full catalogue of books are available at

www.delaneydiamond.com.

ABOUT THE AUTHOR

Delaney Diamond is the USA Today Bestselling Author of sensual, passionate romance novels. Originally from the U.S. Virgin Islands, she now lives in Atlanta, Georgia. She reads romance novels, mysteries, thrillers, and a fair amount of nonfiction. When she's not busy reading or writing, she's in the kitchen trying out new recipes, dining at one of her favorite restaurants, or traveling to an interesting locale.

Enjoy free reads on her website. Join her mailing list to get sneak peeks, notices of sale prices, and find out about new releases.

Join her mailing list
www.delaneydiamond.com

facebook.com/DelaneyDiamond

twitter.com/DelaneyDiamond

bookbub.com/authors/delaney-diamond

pinterest.com/delaneydiamond

goodreads.com/delaney_diamond

www.ingramcontent.com/pod-product-compliance
Lightning Source LLC
Chambersburg PA
CBHW071303250626
47159CB00004B/1288